The Millionaire Murders

EDMOND GAGNON

Edmond Gagnon Author

THE MILLIONAIRE MURDERS

Copyright © 2022 by Edmond Gagnon Author

All rights reserved. No part of this book may be reproduced in any manner whatsoever without written permission except in the case of brief quotations embodied in critical articles and reviews.

Published by Edmond Gagnon Author, Windsor, Ontario, Canada
Printed on acid free paper.
The events, story told, and characters in this book are fictitious. Any similarity to persons living or dead is strictly coincidental and not intended by the author. Any opinions expressed in this book are solely those of the author and do not represent the opinions of others.

First Edition 2022
First Printing, 2022

Editing by Christine Hayton

Cover Design by Christian Laforet

Front Cover Photo courtesy of Paul Sancya, Associated Press

Rear Cover Photo by Edmond Gagnon Author

Other Books by Edmond Gagnon

Norm Strom Crime Series
Rat
Bloody Friday
Torch
Finding Hope
Border City Chronicles
Trafficking Chen

Abigail Brown Crime Series
The Moon Mask
The Millionaire Murders

Others
Four – A Paranormal Thriller
A Casual Traveler
(A Collection of Short Travel Stories)

Website: www.edmondgagnon.com

1
Shot

Albert Pearson tried to focus on the disappearing yellow line that marked the center of the two-lane road. Wet snowflakes splattered on his windshield like a swarm of locust, obscuring his view of the pavement ahead. The late October squall was neither normal nor unusual for that area of Northern Michigan. The fresh white dusting was fine by him. The deer would be easier to track. His cabin sat on a quiet country road less than thirty minutes from the Interstate.

He stopped in Grayling to pick up groceries and booze for the boys' hunting weekend. It was the one and only time of year he invited his closest corporate cronies to his personal hideaway. Pearson went by himself during the spring and summer to fish or relax. The store clerk was busy serving another customer and didn't seem to notice him, but a fifth of Woodford Reserve Kentucky Bourbon greeted the city slicker when he put his groceries on the counter. Judging by the accumulation of dust on the liquor bottle, Pearson was the only customer who drank that particular brand.

They engaged in polite conversation while the owner bagged his supplies. The blinding snow came at him sideways, keeping him off balance on the walk to his SUV. Pearson switched his wipers and defroster to high, thankful for the four-wheel-drive in the Land Rover and the less than ten-minute drive ahead of him. He managed to stay on the road by following tracks left by other vehicles. A long row of snow-laden cedars marked the laneway to his cabin.

Considering the inclement weather, he decided to bring the groceries in first and start a fire to warm things up. About halfway between his SUV and the front porch, Pearson noticed what appeared to be footprints in a path from his cabin to the bush. He paused and let his eyes follow the faint tracks. That's when he felt it. A sharp pain in his lower spine stole his breath. He felt warm and sticky liquid on the back of one hand. Pearson tried to suck air into his lungs. He sensed falling, but he couldn't feel his legs. He saw the bags drop to the ground in slow motion, his upper body following the same path.

There was a sound of glass breaking but he didn't feel the impact when he landed on top of the groceries. The man lay twisted, the left side of his face buried in the snow. It happened so fast. Why didn't his arms break the fall? His reaction was to get up, but his limbs didn't respond. The sharp pain became a burning sensation in his lower abdomen. Pearson thought of calling for help but his phone was in the SUV.

He caught movement out of the corner of his eye; a shadow at first, then a pair of men's boots, the toes pointing at him. Thinking one of his buddies had arrived, he asked for a hand up. A rifle butt landed in the snow, close enough for him to see it clearly. It looked just like his .308 Winchester; his initials, AP, carved in the wood, along with a number he didn't recognize. It was his gun. Pearson tried to turn his head and identify who was standing over him but he could see no further than the man's waist. Whoever the person was, he pivoted in his own tracks.

Pearson assumed the bourbon bottle had broken since the snow around him was slushy and red. He flicked his eyelids to clear snow and realized the red slush looked more like blood than whiskey. Badly injured and bleeding, he felt no pain. Albert Pearson was able to move his head but the rest of his body wouldn't cooperate. He repeatedly called out for help but got no response.

The sound of crunching footfalls in the snow faded, and the stranger disappeared.

2
Stabbed

Doug Cowper stopped the police van on Monroe, across the street from the Greektown Hotel. He gazed past the crime scene tape strung across the alley dividing the Catholic and Orthodox churches. A young patrolwoman who was about to wave him on, recognized his vehicle, and stood fast. The veteran forensics technician grabbed his camera and stepped out onto the pavement.

He walked to the opposite side of the street and snapped a few shots of the general area and mouth of the alley where the victim lay in wait. Cowper questioned the uniformed cop but she knew nothing, her assignment was to guard the scene. He signed her log sheet and eyed his line of approach to avoid contaminating the scene. The hotel side of the street held ample lighting but only shadows and darkness marked the alley entrance. The fresh-faced female cop lifted the tape, allowing the specialist to enter the crime scene. He turned and took a few more images to capture the perspective from the alley to the street, and the hotel. A dust devil picked up debris from the broken pavement behind him and flung it out onto the sidewalk.

The alley resembled a black hole, sucking in any light from the street. Cowper used a flashlight to find his way. He swept it from side to side as he moved, making sure not to disturb any potential evidence. There were voices ahead.

Another beam crossed his; two light sabers engaging in battle. It was one of the cops who should have met him at the tape and guided him into the crime scene.

Cowper bit his tongue, knowing any remarks he made would probably fall on deaf ears. The human carnage that street cops, especially veterans, saw on a daily basis, desensitized them over time. This was just another body in an alley. He continued to sweep the alley with his flashlight, purposely taking in the only other live men on the scene. The older cop's face was familiar, someone who was way beyond accepting any advice from someone like him. The younger rookie appeared fresh out of the academy and should have known better. Protecting and preserving the crime scene was one of the first things taught about homicide investigation. The veteran took the last drag off a cigarette and flicked the butt deeper into the dark.

Cowper found the victim before either officer said anything useful. He stepped closer to the body and took the initiative. "What've we got, officers?"

The lopsided grin on the senior cop's face said he regarded forensic specialists as lab techs, who didn't have the balls to work the front lines. "Probably one of the hotel guests from across the street...came over here for a smoke and got stuck by a crackhead looking for drug money...no wallet or ID."

Officer Cowper was an acting sergeant and technically outranked both uniformed cops, but they didn't work for him. A reserved man, thin-framed and balding gracefully, he normally kept his opinions to himself. The litter-strewn alley wasn't deserving of a paper body suit and booties, but it was still a crime scene, with potential evidence to collect. He snapped at the older cop. "Thank you for the narrative.

Do you think the cigarette butts around the body are his...or yours?"

The veteran took pause to come up with an answer.

Two new voices at the mouth of the alley disrupted their silence. Silhouettes offered clues Cowper quickly put together. The man who was almost as wide as he was tall, carried a valise and wore a black windbreaker sporting the words, Medical Examiner. The taller and much slimmer figure with him had all the proper female curves. The foul language she spewed left him with no doubt. It was Detective Abigail Brown.

In the dark alley, crisscrossing beams from police flashlights resembled searchlights from the nearby Greektown Casino. Eventually, they all converged on a casually dressed white male, laying in a puddle of his own blood.

Detective Brown cleared her throat. "Hey Skel, what the hell are you doing out after dark, I thought you were a nine-to-fiver now that you're a supervisor?"

Because of his boney physique, Cowper got the nickname early in his career, based on the cartoon character, Skelator, from the Masters of the Universe. "Hello, Abigail, nice to see you too."

The medical examiner dropped to one knee and looked over the body.

Brown glanced at the uniforms, rolled her eyes, and resumed her conversation with Cowper. "What can you tell me so far?"

"Not much, I've only been here a few minutes and they haven't been much help." He tilted his head toward the two patrolmen. "No ID, maybe a robbery."

Abigail turned to the uniformed cops. "Who called it in?"

They searched each other for the answer. The rookie spoke. "Dispatch said it was someone from the Catholic Church."

She barked. "Well then maybe you should get your asses over there and find out who that was and get a statement. You know...like real cops do on TV. Then hit the hotel and start canvassing."

The old cop grumbled. "There's like eighty-something rooms in there."

"Then you better get fucking started, officer, if you want to get home for breakfast."

Cowper took photographs. Abigail normally snapped a few images of her own but she knew how thorough her forensic friend was, and that he'd send her copies.

The ME rolled the victim over so he could check the core temperature and estimate time of death. "Male, Caucasian, fifty-five to sixty, casual but tailored clothes...I count seven visible puncture wounds, four to the abdomen and three defensives on the left hand and arm—a narrow blade, probably a pocket knife. It's odd though."

"What's that?" Brown asked.

"There should be more blood from that many wounds...must have missed the vital organs or he bled internally. His jacket soaked up its share. I'll know more with an autopsy. Current body temp tells me he's only been dead a couple hours."

Abigail responded. "Thanks, Doc." Brown turned to find Cowper working his way deeper into the alley. She walked up behind him. "Did you see the scuff marks on top of his shoes?"

"Yeah, I'm checking for a blood trail to see if the body was moved or he crawled toward the street. There's so much debris in this alley...that old cop walked all over the place and threw cigarette butts wherever he pleased."

"I know the asshole...he's living proof ya can't teach an old dog new tricks. I heard wife number three dumped him and he can't afford to retire."

"And what are you doing here, Abigail, since when does Major Crimes handle random muggings or stabbings?"

"Random? Is that your expert opinion, Specialist?"

"Just saying..."

"I know. Things have been slow...not sure why. The brass ordered everyone to take off as much accrued time as they could so the city can meet its budget. So, between the lull in homicides and lack of personnel...I'm out here slumming with you."

Cowper smiled and aimed his camera lens at Brown.

"Okay, okay...I'll leave you to it and go check for witnesses.

3
Night

Abigail Brown didn't consider herself nocturnal, but she enjoyed the peace and quiet the nightshift normally brought with it. Even in a busy city like Detroit, after businesses closed and everyone was tucked in safely at home, most life on the street went into hibernation. But the city was no different from the wilderness and there were always certain creatures prowling the night.

The major case detective stood in the mouth of the alley, facing the hotel across the street. She looked to the left and right, thinking and contemplating, playing out scenarios in her head, trying to imagine events ending with a dead man in the alley. Brown sucked in a deep breath, held it for a second, and blew out from puffed cheeks. She had nothing useful.

The air was cool, normal for that time of night in early June. She caught the scent of rusty metal and sulfur, probably from the steam spewing from a manhole cover nearby. Wings fluttered overhead. Abigail traced the bird's path back to its roost on top of a gargoyle, standing guard over the Catholic Church entrance. The stone creature laughed at her presence.

The detective's phone rang. It was Jamila Harris, her new lieutenant. They called her Jamila the Hun, because of her aggressive and micro-managing style. "Do you need me out there, Detective?" It was her way of checking up and offering unwanted advice. She worked steady days, but was notified of all homicides in her precinct, and called in if needed.

"It's a no-brainer. Hotel guest wandered into the wrong alley. I'll have my report on your desk before you arrive in the morning."

"I could be there in twenty minutes...forensics and ME on scene?" There it was, the Hun doing her thing. Most would do it for the overtime but Harris yearned for the chance to throw her weight around. She carried a considerable amount of it.

"Everyone's where they should be, boss, thanks for asking."

"Alright, Detective, I trust your judgement."

That must have been a joke; Jamila Harris trusted no one. Brown hung up the phone and heard a commotion in front of the Greektown Hotel. A hysterical woman was being restrained by a uniformed cop. The detective walked across the street and under the canopy covering the entrance to the hotel. Eyeing the sobbing female, Abigail assumed she was about to meet the victim's widow.

The woman told the detective, she and her husband, Joel Humboldt, were staying at the hotel. They fought and he went for a walk to cool off. Brown led Mrs. Humboldt into the hotel lobby. They went over everything from earlier in the evening. The couple lived in Farmington Hills, and decided to stay the night after having dinner and too many drinks. Everything went well, until a discussion over her husband's business turned sour.

From his physical description and clothing, Detective Brown was sure the victim was Joel Humboldt. When the wife broke down crying again, Abigail texted Cowper and asked if he could send her a photo of the victim to confirm identity. To distract the grief-stricken woman, Brown asked if she could take a quick look around her hotel room.

Once inside, Mrs. Humboldt went directly to the bathroom and vomited. Abigail wasn't sure if it was from grief or alcohol. The woman reeked of booze. There were two wine bottles on the table, one empty and the other almost. The rest of the room was tidy, with no signs of a struggle. The lack of luggage confirmed the couple's last-minute decision to spend the night. The detective found nothing suspicious in the room.

When all was quiet in the bathroom, Brown asked the female cop, who came with them, to check on the woman. She considered Mrs. Humboldt as she exited the bathroom. She resembled the walking dead. Brown asked if there was anyone, they could call but the widow claimed she needed sleep, and would take care of all that later. Mrs. Humboldt dropped onto the bed and passed out.

Abigail returned to the crime scene, before heading back to the office. The black curtain of night had started its retreat. Layers of indigo and burnt orange heralded the new day. After being up all night, sunrise was difficult to manage. Gravity worked at her eyelids. Since she had paperwork to complete; she stopped to grab a coffee. It would give her the jolt she needed to finish her report before the lieutenant arrived for the day shift. The hot black liquid was a stinging reminder Abigail was still alive.

Too bad Joel Humboldt couldn't say the same.

4
Speared

Mark Bulmer was as giddy as a kid on the first day of summer break. The month of June on the water was unpredictable in Michigan, but the day was perfect to take his baby out for a cruise. He spent the previous weekend cleaning and readying the Bayliner after its long winter slumber.

The corporate CEO climbed aboard his pride and joy, threw his day bag on the passenger seat, and placed a small cooler behind him. He fired up the engines and listened to them purr in harmony. Ready to go, he aimed his yacht, the *Surrender*, at Lake St. Clair. Bulmer christened the powerboat after a corporate acquisition that supplied him with more than enough cash to reward himself.

He released the mooring lines and stepped behind the wheel as the vessel drifted into the canal leading to the lake. Bulmer nudged the gear lever ahead a notch and engaged the transmission. His just reward lurched forward heading for open water. Wearing a smile befitting man of the year, he scanned the collection of boats in the marina, confident his was the biggest and the best.

Coming up to a buoy marking the lake channel, Bulmer placed a Cohiba between his lips and lit up. That first drag was always the best; almost as good as sex...almost. Gazing through the cloud of exhaled smoke at the smooth water ahead, the corporate raider replayed his last takeover in his head. Man, he was good.

He pushed the drive lever ahead another notch and marveled at how the engines growled in response. There were very few other boats on the lake. Working-class stiffs were busy toiling away to pay for their wet dreams. Bulmer grinned. He'd been there and done that, but being the top dog had its perks, and he took time off as he pleased. Today's adventure was a good decision because the weatherman was right, for a change. Nothing but blue sky and calm water lay ahead.

Testing the engines, Bulmer called for more power. The bow cut through the swell of a nearby lake freighter like a hot knife through cream cheese. He scoffed at the rolling wave. He was really cruising now. A glance over his shoulder to check the Surrender's impressive wake left Bulmer imagining he was Moses, parting the Red Sea.

The snap of a metal latch below deck made him wonder if he closed the door to the head properly. Turning his attention away from the wheel, he noticed the cabin door was ajar. That's when a blur of flying metal sliced into his ribcage. He instinctively grabbed the steel shaft of the projectile fired from the spear gun he kept below deck. Bulmer liked to play with this toy when he was out fishing. He couldn't believe someone just shot him with his own weapon. The pain was unbearable.

A stranger emerged from the cabin, grabbed him by one arm, and rolled him out of his seat. Bulmer's legs gave out and he ended up on the floor near the stern. The shooter reached over and adjusted the throttle, slowing the boat to a crawl. Mark Bulmer asked his attacker who he was and why he shot him. There was no response. He wondered how the intruder got onto his boat unnoticed and what he planned next. Who was this man and why was he doing this?

The stranger fussed with the antique life preserver and the anchor line. His attention diverted; Bulmer pulled his cell phone from his pants pocket. Blood covered the phone, as well as his shirt and pants. The shooter turned and saw Bulmer thumbing the buttons. He moved astern, grabbed the phone, and tossed it overboard. The wounded company executive was next. His assailant rolled him off the back deck like a depth charge. He took in a mouthful of water and went under a few feet, but bobbed back up to the surface. Horrified, Bulmer had no idea what was happening to him.

The Surrender drifted away. His assailant flung the life preserver overboard. Struggling to keep his head above water, Bulmer reached for the antique float; his vessel's name stenciled on it. He grabbed hold. The stranger circled the boat around him and pulled away, taking up the slack in the rope. Bulmer realized the line was wrapped around his shoulders. Before he could get a hand inside it, the loop slid up and tightened around his neck. Fear took hold and he knew the man was trying to kill him. The Surrender dragged Bulmer like bait on a trolling line.

The cold water numbed the pain from the spear wound. The corporate raider sucked lake water instead of air into his lungs. The boat picked up speed and his head slipped below the surface. Bulmer loved being on the lake his whole life and was a good swimmer. He had no fear of the water. The last thing he saw was the emptiness above that awaited him.

5
Floater

Ackley Scott plopped a cup of liquid caffeine on Abigail's desk, and stood fast for some morning chitchat. He had been Brown's partner for a short while, until a fellow police officer shot him by mistake. His injury kept him off the street and out of the detective rotation, but the brass kept him in Major Crimes, where his keen computer skills served best.

"What took you so long?"

"Starbucks was lined up out the door with people ordering candy-flavored rocket fuel like yours...it's all expresso and chocolate in there."

Brown glanced up, giving Ackley a quick once-over. He was young and smart. His meagre physique, wavy hair, and wire-rimmed glasses made him look more like John Lennon than a cop. The padded shoulders in his tailored suits made him feel like he belonged in the Major Crimes Unit. "I need the jolt...one of us had to work last night."

"Cost me six bucks, it would be cheaper to feed you a line of cocaine. I would have come in to help but they don't trust me working with you after dark."

"Don't remind me. My partners have a habit of getting shot."

Scott blew through the hole in his cup's lid to cool the steaming brew. "Do you think that's why they haven't teamed you with anyone since Perez bought it at the liquor store?"

"I dunno...they haven't brought me into the loop, I'm only..."

The Hun suddenly appeared, filling the office door. She handed a note to Abigail. Jamila Harris was new to Major Crimes and replaced Lieutenant Robinson. A former sergeant in narcotics, she was promoted and transferred to Homicide after she turned in one of her own crew. "They found a body in Lake St. Clair. Coast Guard towed the boat and the vic to the Crescent Sail Yacht Club in Grosse Pointe. Department of Public Safety called for our assistance."

Detective Brown replied. "The DPS can't handle a fucking floater?"

Her former boss would have chastised Abigail for her use of vulgarity, but Harris grew up in the projects and was tough as nails. Foul language bothered her about as much as the coffee stain on the front of her untucked blouse. "I'm sure they can, Crunch, but the floater's a VIP here in the D, and that makes it a Major Crimes investigation." Harris called Abigail, 'Crunch' as in Captain Crunch, because of her reputation for taking down *serial* killers.

Ackley cut in. "Someone rich and shameless, LT?"

"Mark Bulmer."

Brown and Scott eyeballed each other, and shrugged in unison.

"Really? You should read the news once in a while. He's a media mogul...owns all the major newspapers in Michigan."

Abigail protested. "I was just about to head to the morgue for the autopsy on last night's stabbing."

"Soup and Square Head can handle the morgue and interview the widow...besides, the vic's not going anywhere.

You can catch up with them and read the coroner's report later. Bulmer's a priority and I want to get on it before the media does. The chief will want answers. Take Hacker with you, I'm tired of seeing him mope around the office." Hacker was the moniker she used for Scott. She gave everyone in the office a nickname; something she carried over from narcotics.

"I thought I wasn't allowed in the field?"

"It's a dead body Hacker, they don't shoot back. Get some fresh air...if the floater doesn't smell too bad." The Lieutenant chuckled and waddled away before Brown or Scott could offer a rebuttal.

Their new boss proved capable so far. She didn't take any shit from those above her, and had no problem dishing it out to those below. Except for the cop she turned in, they liked her in narcotics. That's where she got the name Jamila the Hun, after the ancient ruler who was feared by even the Romans.

Scott winced and excused himself. He did the poop-walk while Brown googled Mark Bulmer. She giggled. Her ex-partner's bowel movements were as predictable as the clock on the office wall. She thought he might be nervous about going on the road, but it was more likely the black coffee working its magic. She looked at the computer screen.

The LT was right. Bulmer was a media big shot. There were several links to corporate mergers and acquisitions of smaller companies. He had no criminal record in the DPD files. His car was stolen once and he had some outstanding parking fines. *Guess we won't be collecting those,* she thought. There were two addresses listed; an older one in Grosse Pointe, and a more recent one at the Riverfront Towers, in Downtown Detroit.

The homicide detectives cruised along West Jefferson, Scott with his window down and arm hanging outside the car. It was the third day of sunshine with above seasonal temperatures. The odor of river water and spawning fish tainted the air. He gawked at Belle Isle and recalled the family picnics he enjoyed there as a child. He turned to Abigail. "Did you visit the island when you were a kid?"

"A few times. My uncle thought weather like this was more suited to baseball and we spent a lot of the summer cheering for the Tigers. No picnic sandwiches for me, just lots of peanuts and hot dogs. Shit, Ackley, now I'm craving a ballpark frank."

He looked past Brown, to the sprawling houses in Grosse Pointe. "You ever wonder what it's like to own something like that?"

"And spend all my time cleaning, pulling weeds, and cutting fucking grass? Nope."

"When you've got that kind of quid you hire someone to do that stuff. My parents did. The marina should be just ahead on the right."

"Oh, you mean on the water side of the street, Whacker?"

"It's Hacker." Ackley replied while doing his best impression of the Hun. They both laughed…unaware of the human carnage awaiting them.

6
Surrender

A young dude in an orange safety vest recognized the unmarked police car, and waved the city detectives on through, to the waterfront. Department of Public Safety vehicles were parked along the dock. Two Coast Guard vessels and a Detroit Police boat moored near the outer edge of the marina. Detectives Brown and Scott followed the wooden gangway to where all the uniforms were gathered.

The group stood beside a boat bigger than Abigail's apartment. Flabbergasted by the number of police officials on scene, she wondered if the whole DPS were there. Smells of diesel fuel and rotting fish hung heavy in the air. Scott walked straight to a uniformed police officer who had his back to them, and flicked the back of his head with a finger.

The cop spun around with his arm half-cocked, ready to throw of punch. His scowl turned to a grin. "Hackerman! How are ya, cousin?"

It seemed everyone had a nickname for Scott, even his extended family.

"Busy, D-David, but more than happy to show you how to solve a homicide. What came out as a stutter was Ackley's attempt at coming up with a suitable moniker for his cousin. He failed. That's quite the yacht...someone smuggling dope from Canada and overdosed on their own product before making delivery?"

A salt-and-pepper-haired man wearing a designer suit overheard Scott's comment and threw him a stare capable of flash freezing a holiday turkey. Cousin David introduced the Detroit detective to his chief. A bit embarrassed, Ackley only offered a shrug. He turned his head away to the empty space beside him, where his partner had been a moment earlier. Another officer leaned in and whispered something into the chief's ear. Scott took the opportunity to catch up with his partner.

Abigail had slipped around the cousins and made her way to the vessel's stern. She was climbing aboard when he caught up. He was on her six when the DPS forensics specialist pointed to the waterlogged body on the swimming platform at the back of the Surrender. The city homicide dicks took in the grizzly sight. Ackley pinched his nostrils, trying to avoid the stench of rotting flesh. Abigail's mind flashed back to the bloated women's bodies they pulled out of the Detroit River about a year earlier. She changed the channel in her brain and turned to the CSI.

"What's with the life buoy...is that how you lassoed the vic to get him aboard?"

"We haven't figured that out yet, looks like he got tangled and maybe strangled by the rope. And you'll want to see this...." The specialist reached down, pointing to a hole in the man's abdomen. "It's a puncture wound. I've done some scuba diving and I believe this was inflicted by a spear gun."

Abigail threw her head back in surprise. "Really...that's a new one, can't say I've ever come across one of those on the street. And what about the marks on his neck...rope burns from the life preserver?"

"That's my thinking too. And if..." He looked to Abigail as if asking for permission to continue.

"By all means, enlighten me."

"Well, Detective, it appears he was dragged behind the boat. Notice how one of his shoes is missing and how his pants are partially pulled down. Our Medical Examiner has already been here and gone. Without the autopsy, we can't tell if he was strangled, bled out, or drowned. We both agree foul play was involved and he didn't simply fall overboard. The victim owns the vessel."

Scott snooped around while his partner took a closer look at the body. He shook his head at the opulence of the luxury craft. It reminded him of a smaller version of the ship his parents took him on for a Caribbean cruise. A crime scene tech who was packing up his kit, told him the vessel was spotless, with the exception of a couple drops of blood and fingerprints that likely belonged to the victim.

Ackley sat in the captain's seat, trying to imagine what it would be like to operate such a majestic watercraft. He couldn't. Although a whiz with computers, the nautical gauges and dials didn't mean anything to him. He took note of the GPS and flicked it on to see if there was a map. A series of numbers showed up. He assumed they were coordinates and jotted them down.

Abigail tapped her partner on the shoulder and asked if he was done playing. She said that the DPS Captain started a jurisdictional pissing match over who'd interview the ex-wife so she agreed one of theirs would come with. "Let's get out of here before he tries to prove who's got the bigger dick."

7
B

Detectives Lynda Campbell and Karl Knudsen made the short drive from Police Headquarters to the Greektown Hotel, to obtain an official statement from Darlene Humboldt. Lieutenant Harris said Detective Brown was needed elsewhere, and assigned them the follow-up. Campbell rolled her eyes when the boss referred to them as Soup and Square Head. She skimmed Abigail's report and learned the victim, Joel Humboldt, was well off. He'd inherited a chain of muffler and lube shops, expanding and absorbing the competition to become the largest auto repair company in the state. According to the report, the victim was stabbed to death in the alley across from the Greektown Hotel.

After getting no answer at Mrs. Humboldt's room, hotel management told the B Team she checked out during the night. The detectives shared a glance but weren't surprised. They both knew how unpredictable grieving people could be. The pair of investigators worked well together, even though they had different investigative styles and backgrounds prior to joining the police department.

Campbell earned her stripes in the major case unit during the Henry Jensen serial killer case led by her friend, Abigail Brown. The two of them grew close during the investigation, but soon after drifted apart. Reconnecting with her was something on the top of Lynda's to do list.

She normally drew meathead or macho male partners. Knudsen was more the latter, but with a good sense of humor. A veteran of Afghanistan, the former Special Forces soldier was a monster of a street cop. He had a good reputation, but was somewhat of a racist when it came to dealing with anyone from the Middle East. After complaints about his behavior, he moved to Intelligence, where he worked on a terrorist task force run by the State Police. Frustrated with being a data collector and file clerk, Knudsen put in for a transfer to major crimes, where he could actually see the fruits of his labor. He still sported a military-style haircut, thus earning him the moniker Square Head. He spoke highly of a woman he worked with in Special Forces and had no problem with a female partner.

She took in the ex-soldier's profile while he stared out the passenger window. Karl was the first male partner who let her drive. He reminded her of the Rockem-Sockem Robots her brother had as a child. The robots had big square heads, protruding jaws, and blonde buzz cuts. Campbell never saw him shirtless, but his tight clothes and V-shaped upper body left little to her imagination. The man was a hunk, but not her type.

Knudsen turned to her and ran a hand over the shiny bristles on his head. "What's your take on this, partner...simple robbery gone bad?"

They'd decided to see the coroner first, to get some answers before they visited the widow. "Seems that way, we'll know more shortly." Campbell parked in one of the 'Police Vehicles Only' spots at the City Morgue.

Detective Knudsen marveled at the Medical Examiner's work. It reminded him of a butcher carving the perfect porterhouse steak. His partner did an about face when the man's rib cage was spread open like a pair of louvered doors. She turned her attention to a side table, and the bag of personal belongings collected from the victim; a man's belt, package of cigarettes, cheap lighter, a roll of quarters, and a gold wedding band. They were not exactly the things you would expect to see on a robbery victim. She wondered if the ring was too hard to remove, or in his haste, the killer simply didn't see it. The roll of quarters would have been particularly hard to miss, unless the killer mistook it for a part of the man's anatomy.

Karl called Lynda back to the examination table and she stuffed the victim's belongings back into the evidence bag. The ME pointed to the puncture wounds one at a time, explaining how each of them missed vital organs, almost as if done intentionally. The Doctor felt it was unusual in a hurried or vicious attack. The detectives exchanged a curious look, not sure of the findings or what conclusion they should draw.

Knudsen bitched about the trip all the way to Farmington Hills, saying Mrs. Humboldt should have come into the station for a formal interview and shouldn't receive special treatment just because she was rich. Her lawyer and their captain made the arrangements. On arrival, seeing the newly widowed woman was distraught and she appeared to be of Middle Eastern descent, Campbell handled the interview.

Her partner asked to use the restroom so he could snoop around the house, but the lawyer was present and watched his every move. After the usual questions about possible marital or money problems and suspected enemies, Detective Campbell asked if they could take a quick look at the victim's home office. The lawyer said they were welcome to, after they obtained a legal search warrant.

The investigators got the same response when they asked to examine his work place and to interview Humboldt's employees. After receiving a sarcastic remark from Knudsen about the lawyer's lack of cooperation in his client's death, the legal eagle said he would make people available only if arrangements went through him.

8
Autistic

Detective Brown pointed the unmarked car west and drove towards the city. "I'm hungry. You wanna stop at Wigley's in the Eastern Market for a sandwich, on the way downtown?"

"Jesus, Abigail, how can you be hungry after looking at a smelly rotting body? I can still smell it on me and my clothes."

"I guess I've gotten desensitized from all the death and destruction I've seen in the war and on our own streets. It's just never really bothered me. When I was a kid, I used to sneak into my uncle's bedroom and look through his scrapbooks of photos taken during the race riots. Bodies were left to burn on the street."

"Nice. I was happy finding my dad's skin magazines. That reminds me, can we stop at a bookshop on Woodward? I'd like to drop by to see my little brother, and maybe bring him a sandwich. He loves corned beef."

"The retarded kid from Big Brothers?"

"Christ, Abigail, we don't use that word...he's mentally challenged, but still special in lots of ways. Justin is a whiz with puzzles and he can solve complex equations in his head. He has more computing power in his brain than any hardware I've ever used."

"Coming from a geek like you, that says a lot. Sorry."

Abigail exited the freeway, and headed toward the market. "They've got good soup, maybe it will settle your stomach. You should blow your nose. The smell sticks to the little hairs in there and whatever you eat will smell like rotting flesh."

"Good to know...you think they have chicken noodle?"

"Beat's me...is that your favorite?"

"That's what my mother fed me whenever I felt ill or had a stomach ache. Hey, speaking of soup, what's going on with you and Campbell? I thought you two were besties."

"I'm not sure. We drifted apart when she left and shacked up with the Indian. Could be work...different cases...her new partner. My fault too, I guess. I'm so easily consumed when focused on a big case."

Ackley was in luck. They had his favorite soup. He did his best to enjoy it but couldn't shake the smell of death from his nasal passages. Abigail tried to wrap her lips around a corned beef sandwich twice the size of her mouth. Juice dripped down her chin. Ackley chuckled and handed her a napkin. He ordered a sandwich to go.

Abigail parked in front of the bookstore and they got out of the car. "What does your little brother do in there?"

"His official title is stock boy. He keeps the shelves tidy and shuffles books around to make room for new arrivals. Justin can tell you exactly where every title is located. He's a voracious reader and remembers everything he consumes...Detroit News, Free Press, New York Times, Time magazine, even the dictionary."

"He has a photographic memory?"

"Not exactly. He has a type of autism but he learned how to function in the real world. It's all about routine. He has a series of steps he repeats constantly, to get him through the day."

A handsome young man with cropped hair and stubby ears wheeled a cart full of books across the lobby as the detectives walked in the front door. Justin glanced at his brother and smiled, but kept walking and turned down one of the isles.

Abigail flipped her brow. "I guess he's too busy to stop and visit."

Ackley walked toward the back of the store where his little brother had disappeared. "We have to go to him; he can't disrupt his routine."

She followed her partner to where the kid was busy slipping books into empty slots on a shelf. He didn't acknowledge their presence until Ackley spoke. "Hey, Justin, have you had lunch yet? I brought you a corned beef sandwich...with Dijon mustard...just the way you like it."

The young man continued working. "It's not lunch time."

"I understand, maybe you can eat it on your afternoon break?"

"2:15 to 2:35. I eat fruit and yogurt."

Ackley nodded in submission. "Okay, Justin. I'll put it in the lunchroom fridge for you to eat later. Hey, I want to introduce you to my partner, Abigail Brown."

Justin paused and turned to Abigail. His eyes never met hers, they looked to a place somewhere beyond her, but he spoke as if he knew the woman. "Detective Abigail Brown, Homicide, Major Crimes, Detroit Police...captured serial killers Henry Jensen and Samantha Evans...cited personally by the former chief and mayor. Ackley says you're hot."

Caught off guard by the recap of his partner's career, and embarrassed by the last part, he turned to Abigail. Seeing the wide eyes and crooked smile she sported, he wasn't sure if she was shocked or impressed. "It's nice to meet you Justin, your big brother speaks highly of you...and me too, apparently."

Ackley told the young man he'd let him get back to work and would give his sandwich to the store manager who could put it in the fridge for him.

Without breaking routine, Justin picked up another book from the cart and scanned the cover. "Border City Chronicles by Edmond Gagnon...Crime fiction...Isle eleven...fourth shelf...eighteenth from the left...between Finding Hope and Moon Mask. Bye Detectives Ackley Scott and Abigail Brown." Justin grabbed his cart and pushed it down the aisle, disappearing around a corner.

9
Burned

Norbert Lee walked out of the car dealership and climbed into his one-year-old Bentley SUV. He wasn't a sports utility vehicle kind of guy, but his wife had taken a shine to the fancy ride. He had just ordered the latest and more expensive model of Rolls Royce. The sticker price wasn't negotiable but that didn't matter. Money was no object now. He owned the rights to all present and future *Wired Electronics* stores in Michigan, Ohio, and Indiana.

The business tycoon started the engine and shifted into reverse. His phone rang so he braked and the Bentley jerked to a stop. Lee heard a thump behind him. He answered the call and checked his rearview mirror, thinking he'd backed into something. There was nothing to see. His company vice president called to report his imagined crisis of the day. Lee removed a cigarette case from his pocket and lit one up. He sucked on the filtered cancer stick and filled his lungs with smoke, while his second in command whined and complained about the latest dilemma. The boss held his tongue, all the while wondering why the well-paid executive couldn't make a decision without running it by him first.

Years of smoking dulled Lee's sense of smell, but he detected the odor of gasoline in his SUV. He glanced around the dealership lot, thinking there must be some kind of fuel spill. His pants felt wet, as if he'd sat in something.

Hearing, but not really listening to what his VP was babbling on about, Lee pinched the cigarette between his lips and reached down with his free hand to feel the seat.

He brought the wet hand to his nose and grabbed the cigarette. It lit up like a dry Christmas tree. *WHOOF*—the gas fumes and liquid contained in his vehicle ignited. The back seat burst into flames. Lee panicked and dropped the phone. Instinctively he rolled down his window, but that only fed the hungry fire with a fresh supply of oxygen. While blue and orange flames consumed the plush velour lining around him, the business mogul reached for the door latch. Lee's brain told him to get out of the car, but his limbs didn't respond fast enough. He grabbed the metal handle; hot as the business end of a fire poker. He turned and tried to climb over the center console, heading for the passenger door. The raging fire beat him to it.

His clothes on fire, Lee swatted the flames. In a fit of desperation, he tried to kick out the passenger window. The glass gave way supplying even more fuel to the raging inferno. It consumed him. Flesh burned and melted before his eyes. He screamed in pain and cried for help. The heat and smoke were blinding. He saw people outside, trying to extinguish the fire.

In his last act of self-preservation, Norbert Lee unconsciously tucked himself into the fetal position. He could smell his burnt flesh, but no longer felt any pain. Thinking that he was about to die, his last thought was of his wife. He truly loved her and hoped she never found out about the affair.

10
Caseload

Lieutenant Harris popped out of her aquarium and yelled for Bulldog and Sleeper. She could walk across the room to personally deliver the message, but liked to let everyone know the boss was in. "Get over to World Class Cars out on Plymouth Road for a crispy critter...ME and Forensics are on the way."

As partners, Bruce Dunn and Harry Cummings had about as much in common as night and day. Dunn was blue-black in color, short and stocky, with a tight afro and two chipped front teeth—half the reason Harris labelled him Bulldog. She brought him with her from narcotics because of the other reason. When he sank his teeth into something, he never let go. He was also a former Olympic sprinter.

Cummings, however, was his partner's polar opposite. A pasty-skinned white man whose towering height and barrel-shaped upper body left him hunched. Older than dinosaur excrement, he suffered from narcolepsy, alcoholism, and constant pain in his back from a piece of shrapnel he collected in Viet Nam. The decorated war veteran was well-past retirement age but rumor was someone upstairs owed him, and was keeping him there.

It was late in the afternoon and almost quitting time. The lieutenant heard Cummings grumbling from the back of the room. "You awake, Sleeper? I know it's past your bedtime. Maybe you can get out there while the case is still hot." She chuckled. "Pun intended. And check out the gawkers...some torches like to hang around and admire their handy work." A combination of ghetto and southern drawl took the humor out of her sarcasm.

Bulldog was already at the door offering his partner a scowl that said, *hurry the fuck up old man.*

Harris glanced around the room at the other detectives, busy working on their laptops and completing reports. "I know it's been a bit slow around here, DEFECTIVES, so why does the unsolved side of the board have so many more names than the solved? Let's close some cases people. You know how the captain is about the stats and our case load."

Ackley Scott's desk resembled the launch control center at Houston, with a semicircle of computer screens at his beckon. He went over his notes with Abigail Brown, trying to finish the reports on their floater from the lake. Ackley searched his partner's expression, in response to the lieutenant's speech. She rolled her eyes and leaned in for a closer look at something.

"Hey, what are those numbers you copied from the GPS on the boat?"

"Navigation coordinates, I think...haven't checked them out yet."

In Afghanistan, Abigail spent most of her time in logistics. "Let me see...3085...too clean for longitude or latitude...no spaces, directions, or decimal points. Last four digits of a phone number? Something to do with the boat? Any other ideas, Hacker?"

"I really hate that name you know. Your Spidey sense telling you the numbers are a clue? That seems like a stretch."

Abigail flipped back through the pages of her notes, to the murder in the alley.

"My stabbing vic had a roll of quarters in in his pocket. I thought that was strange at the time, but I've seen weirder things. You're right...it's a stretch."

"Maybe the coins were for the slots at Greektown Casino. There are forty coins in a roll... two less digits than the boat's number. I can run them through the computer, but they're just random numbers and won't amount to anything without some kind of search parameters."

"Wasted thoughts...don't worry about it. Let's concentrate on the evidence we have. Who were the vics, and all the usual suspects? We have to consider the wives. There's money involved. Given the number of stab wounds, it could be a crime of passion. Get what you can on the floater. I'm going back to my desk to work on the stabbing."

Abigail walked by Lynda's desk and thought about stopping to chat but didn't have anything to say. Campbell, buried in her paperwork, caught a familiar scent of perfume. She raised her head and watched the graceful gait of her good friend walking away. Her train of thought broken, she wondered how and why the two of them drifted apart.

Knudsen unintentionally cleared his throat. Lynda glanced at her partner, and went back to the witness statement she'd been reading. The detectives filed their follow-up reports on the Humboldt homicide. Brown was the lead investigator, and capable enough to handle it. They had enough of their own cases to work.

11
Runner

Bruce Dunn threw the car into park before its wheels stopped. His partner was napping and he was quite proud of how abruptly he woke the old man. The younger detective stood beside the burnt-out shell of a newer model Bentley, long before his partner made it out of their unmarked unit.

Dunn checked the firefighters on scene, searching for their captain. He stood next to a rescue truck, talking to the Medical Examiner. *Great,* the detective thought, *two birds with one stone.* He walked over and slipped into the conversation. The two men talked about the previous night's Tiger game, but went silent when three became a crowd.

The ME didn't have much to say. "Male...overcooked, but appears to be Caucasian, late 50's – early 60's, looks well off from the vehicle he drove. I'll know more after the autopsy, but the cause of death looks pretty obvious." He nodded towards a uniformed cop. "She got his name from the dealership...Nobert Lee, it was his car..."

Before the ME could finish, Dunn headed in the direction of the patrol officer. Cummings appeared frozen in time, like a newly discovered Egyptian mummy. He stared at the charred corpse in the burned-out car. It reminded him of something he'd seen in Nam.

Dunn remembered what his lieutenant said about gawkers, and paused to scan the crowd of onlookers. The young detective saw a white teenager on a bicycle behind his partner, craning his neck for a better look at the human carnage. He moved closer, trying to get the war veteran's attention and point out the kid behind him. The cyclist and the Bulldog made eye contact and the kid turned to leave. Dunn yelled at Cummings to grab him, but the old cop was oblivious.

The former track star broke into a trot when the suspect started to ride away. Not sure he could catch up, the detective called out for him to stop. The kid pedaled faster. Dunn sprinted after the cyclist. Riding his bike along the front of the plaza, the kid headed toward Greenfield Road.

Running at top speed, the detective lost traction in his dress shoes, and wished for his Nikes. He wasn't gaining on the young punk, but his luck changed when the kid got caught in rush-hour traffic. As the cyclist encountered four lanes of cars and trucks, the Bulldog closed the gap. He knew it was wishful thinking but hoped Cummings would use their car to cut off the suspect.

The cyclist zigzagged through traffic as thick as Heinz ketchup, and bounced off a car door in between lanes. Slow-moving and stopped vehicles allowed Dunn to close the gap even more. Once clear of Greenfield Road traffic, the kid picked up speed again. The detective fell behind and worried he might lose the suspect if the kid made it to the freeway ahead.

The police gods granted the cop one more wish. The suspect looked back over his shoulder and unwittingly rode into a pothole. It swallowed his front wheel. He resembled Evil Knevel, flying over the handlebars and crashing headfirst into the pavement. Dunn closed in quickly, afraid the motionless kid was dead.

Just as the detective stopped, reached out, and grabbed an arm, the suspect got up and started to run. Dunn clung to his sleeve, but the kid squirmed right out of the hoodie. Limping badly, he made a break for the freeway. The detective caught up again and tackled him on the cement sidewalk. Dunn kept the suspect pinned to the ground while he reached for his handcuffs. Thinking he'd have to walk the kid all the way back to the crime scene, the detective was grateful when a uniformed cop pulled up.

He wondered if Cummings remained frozen in his own time zone. How long would he have to suffer working with the dinosaur? Dunn got up and brushed himself off. The patrol officer put the suspect in her car and said she was sorry about his suit. It wasn't his best, but it was expensive, and now ruined.

The cop dropped Dunn at the crime scene. The runner was taken to the precinct, where they conducted a brief interview. To their dismay, it was a case of them chasing the kid because he ran, and him running because they were chasing him. There was no evidence he had anything to do with their case, even though as a juvenile, he was charged for setting a garbage bin on fire. As it turned out, the young lad had a thing for watching fires.

The arson investigator on scene confirmed the car, doused with accelerants, ignited when the victim lit a cigarette. Dunn and Cummings would have to wait for the official reports from the Medical Examiner, and come up with a list of potential suspects.

12
Re-read

It was a new day. Their open cases were long past the first forty-eight hours. Lynda Campbell and Karl Knudsen took the remarks made by their supervisor personally. They got an early start and used a table near their desks to line up their open murders for past three months. One by one, the male half of the duo called out vital statistics to his female partner. She used a spreadsheet to list victims' names, race, occupation, place of residence, cause of death, and any other critical evidence. They hoped to find anything overlooked during the initial stages of the investigations. Sometimes it helped to focus on little things that might not have seemed important at the time.

In some cases, forensics, computers, and data collection sites like ViCAP helped investigators by comparing modus operandi in similar crimes across the country. Even with the help of state-of-the-art computers and crime fighting software, diligent work by a dedicated detective would often solve even difficult cases.

Knudsen was out grabbing coffee, when Brown stopped by Campbell's desk. "Hey, Lynda, looks like you've got your work cut out for you." She eyed the Excel document.

"Yeah, trying to avoid the wrath of the Hun...but thought it wise to take another look...see if there's anything we missed the first time around."

"Good for you...maybe she'll like your spread sheet and change your handle to, Excellerator."

"Better than 'Soup'."

They chuckled.

"Hey, I've been meaning to talk to you since you came back from British Columbia. I'm sorry it didn't work out with Two Snakes. I'm no expert on relationships and didn't know what to say."

"I've moved on, I think...been meaning to talk to you too, being he was Norm's friend and all..."

Abigail waved a hand through the air. "That didn't work out either...guess we're both destined to be single. I'm sorry I haven't stayed in touch. You know how wrapped up I get in my work."

"I miss you too!"

"We need to drink some wine, get shit-faced, and man-bash...like the old days."

"I'd love that. How about Friday night, after work? We can order in, drink, and talk till the sun comes up."

"It's a date...my place and I'll supply the wine."

Lynda threw her arms out and Abigail practically fell forward to embrace her. Knudsen walked back into the room and coughed when he got close.

"Sorry, am I interrupting something?"

The two friends held each other at arm's length and laughed. Abigail replied, "Wouldn't you like to know, big boy." She turned to leave.

Karl stood there, unable to speak.

"What is it, partner?"

"We caught a new case...drug overdose up in Highland Park. The uniform on scene says it looks too hinky to be self-induced."

13
Statistics

Ackley Scott may have been one of the walking wounded, but he was still a valuable member of the Major Crimes Unit. He was surprised when his lieutenant let him go with Detective Brown. Technically, he was restricted from going into the field. Considered 'light duty' and with the related liability issues involved, he was normally stuck at his desk.

The young detective missed working the street with Abigail, but he knew his limitations and he was better equipped for office duties. A computer geek since grade school, he was proud of the skills he acquired over the years. Although more suited to a programming job, Scott thought becoming a police officer and donning a uniform, would gain him the respect he desperately sought his entire life.

To spite his overbearing parents, he first applied to the Michigan State Police. After being rejected, but before mom and dad could say, 'we told you so', he applied and was accepted by the Detroit Police.

His patrol sergeant quickly realized Scott was more adept to clerical duties than the front lines. Most cops couldn't type and knew nothing about computers, things that became necessary in modern day policing. With his expertise, Ackley found himself teaching his peers basic software skills, and he worked along with police administrators to bring the department out of the dark ages. His work ethic got him promoted to detective and transferred to sex crimes, where he plied the internet, searching for predators and child pornography. When his boss transferred to major crimes, he brought Scott with him.

One of Ackley's duties was to gather all violent crime stats and enter them into state and federal databases such as ViCAP. Similar modus operandi, weapons, and physical evidence were gathered, tracked, and made accessible to police investigators across the country.

He finished inputting what they had so far on the Mark Bulmer case. When he picked up the Joel Humboldt file, something caught his eye. Both men were millionaires, Bulmer a billionaire. He paused for a minute. Being a statistician, and avid reader of such things, their financial status alone didn't mean much because there were twelve known billionaires in the area, and hundreds more millionaires. Scott glanced over at Abigail's empty desk, and the lieutenant's empty office, wondering if he should bring his discovery to anyone's attention.

Martha Wells interrupted his thinking when she dropped a pile of new files on his desk. He snapped his head up, hoping to say hi, and get his fill of the pretty office clerk he'd been dreaming about forever, but she had already turned away. He knew she was single but out of his league. It couldn't hurt to hope and wish, and maybe someday summon the courage to ask her out.

14
Drugged

Detective's Campbell and Knudsen arrived at the address in Highland Park at the same time as the ME. They were walking up to the front door of the luxury condominium building, when forensics pulled up. The group gathered in the lobby to wait for the elevator. Inside the lift, standing behind everyone else, the Square Head used his hands to make a fart sound. Nobody laughed. He moved away from his partner as if she was the offender.

When the doors opened, the group of investigators advanced down the hall like the Detroit Lions offensive unit. The cop guarding the scene took half a step back and addressed the group. "Hope you don't mind...I took the initiative and called in everyone...thinking this death was suspicious. My partner's gone for coffee. Anyone need anything?"

Campbell made eye contact and nodded. "Thanks, officer, we're good."

The team entered the unit one by one, allowing forensics in first.

Standing his post, the cop pointed inside. "He's there in the living room...Lance Delancey. I've got his other particulars when you're ready for them."

The deceased was bound to a dining room chair with duct tape. A balding white man in his sixties, wearing a beige dress shirt and brown pants, he'd vomited all over himself and the floor.

The cop called out from the doorway. "He owns the condo, and according to the manager...a house in Ann Arbor too."

Detective Knudsen took in the designer furnishings, expensive-looking artwork, and bottle of 1926 McCallum Scotch that was open and left on the dining room table. "Must be friggin' nice...that whisky is worth more than all our salaries put together."

The patrolman spoke up again. "He owns Delta Pharmaceuticals and is mega-rich. His company secretary couldn't reach him and asked the super to check up on him. He found Delancey like this...he's downstairs if you want to talk to him."

Detective Campbell watched the ME check the victim's vitals and temperature. She asked the officer, "Do you know the deceased?"

"No, but my wife worked for one of the companies he took over. Her and other long-time employees are now out of work. He promised no one would lose their jobs. I had to start moonlighting to pay the bills...can't say I'm sorry the rich prick is dead."

The ME scowled. "Thank you, officer, we'll take it from here. Dead for about twelve hours...given the bindings around his wrists and ankles, he didn't take his own life. It appears someone force-fed him his own pills."

The forensics specialist busied himself photographing the victim and the assorted pharmaceuticals on the coffee table nearby. He stopped and tapped Detective Campbell on the shoulder. "Check this out."

Beside a pile of tablets, capsules and empty pill bottles, was the number '849', spelled out in little yellow pills.

"What the heck...did you get a shot of that?"

He nodded. "I'm heading for the other rooms."

Campbell checked her partner and was about to ask him what he thought. Knudsen had his nose in the bottle of scotch. "I hope you didn't touch that."

He rolled his eyes. "Just trying to see what all the fuss is about...you think the killer cracked it open in front of the vic just to piss him off?"

"If we're lucky enough to get prints, I'll answer that. Are you a scotch connoisseur?"

"No, just a sewer—I chase the odd shot with a beer. Some rich dude paid like a million bucks for a bottle of this stuff on a TV auction show."

Campbell asked, "What do you think, Doc?"

"I do enjoy a glass of single malt after dinner, but..."

"I meant the numbers...spelled out in pills."

"No idea. Judging by the amount of vomit and foam around the victim's mouth, I can tell you he ingested a lot of them, but in my opinion, 849 sounds like overkill. I'll know more after I examine his stomach contents. Anything absorbed will show up on the tox screen."

Knudsen checked the bathroom medicine cabinet to see what other kind of goodies Delancey kept. Campbell poked her head in the door on the way back from the master bedroom. "Anything interesting?"

"Some feminine products...like he had female company."

"In the bedroom too...a few accoutrements, but no clothes...it'll be interesting to hear what the wife has to say."

"Lynda, what do you think of this?"

She turned to see her partner wearing a partial hairpiece on top of his buzz cut. It was childish and stupid but she couldn't stop herself from laughing. "Cut it out, you idiot."

15
News

The damn newspapers aren't the informative record they used to be, especially with today's unlimited access to the internet. The Free Press is a shadow of its former self and the News is an uninspiring rag. It's no wonder they merged at one point, trying to keep people interested. Corporate greed separated them again...surely it made sense to some asshole in accounting.

Here's the latest nonsense from the Freep—the stupid nickname for the Press that came from their internet address...our mayor is delighted with the low crime rate. Bullshit politics...his dishonor credits the police because he's the one who blew the city budget by hiring more of them. Duh, supply and demand; more cops mean less crime. Taking advantage of the lull in criminal activity, the asshole is bragging and taking credit for all the wonderful things he says he did for the city...nothing but political clout to stuff in his pocket for the next election. His lowness was quick to jump on the accolades bandwagon when police arrested a serial killer who raped women and dumped their bodies in abandoned and derelict houses. Since it was his idea to tear down the derelict houses, he was indirectly responsible for solving the crimes...and that's exactly the way his people leaked it to the press.

Ah, look who else shares the front page with the city's top fleabag. A story the mayor forgot to mention, probably because it occurred in Grayling. One of Detroit's millionaires was shot and killed outside his cottage by guess who? Now that is something interesting and worth reading. According to the paper, state police aren't saying much. It could be because they have shit to go on, but the sneaky pigs like to hold back certain details from the public. Since there are very few investigative reporters these days, cops have more control over what they release to the media. Albert Pearson shot to death, found by a co-worker, and the investigation is ongoing...no shit, typical police response.

So much the cops don't know. Surely, they were able to identify the rifle as the dead mans. They have to be blind not to see Pearson's initials carved on the wood butt, but they will never figure out what the numbers mean, and they will never find any incriminating evidence at the crime scene or inside the cottage. Conveniently, the fresh snowfall covered my footprints around the body and on the property. They will struggle to find a motive and come up with a suspect. They have no idea who I am and why I killed the arrogant bastard.

There was a time after 911, when I stupidly considered going to war for my country, but I didn't want to eliminate complete strangers for their religious beliefs. But killing is easier than I thought. I acted on impulse when that wealthy prick showed up unexpectedly at the cottage. My hatred of the rich... I fantasized how I would do it. The readily available weapon and secluded location were just too good to pass up.

I loved how the wealthy pizza pirate had no idea why he had to die. I saw it in his pleading eyes as he bled out—those questions—who are you...why have you done this to me? Albert Pearson was an ignorant man who cared more about money than anything else.

And you didn't get to take any of it with you...did you Albert?

16
Mayoral

Captain Zawadski popped out of his office like a groundhog searching for its shadow. He rarely addressed the troops, but first thing Friday morning he materialized in the bullpen with Lieutenant Harris in tow. She called out for everyone's attention and said the captain had something to say. The Hun stepped behind her boss, as if she knew it was her place in the chain of command.

The man in charge of major crimes pointed out everyone should be aware homicides were on the rise. The mayor was aware of that fact. Everyone in the room knew their boss and the city leader golfed together and belonged to the same country club. It was also common knowledge the mayor hated the chief of police and was grooming Zawadski to take over the top spot.

"For those of you who don't know, our latest murder victim, Lance Delancey, was a major supporter of the mayor, and considered a personal friend. His Honor is aware of how important the first forty-eight hours are in a homicide investigation, and he wants to pull out all the stops, and bring his friend's killer to justice. Nobody goes home until we catch the culprit."

Someone at the back of the room, asked about overtime.

"I know the chief has put the kibosh on OT, but the mayor has given me his personal assurance you will be paid for your work."

"And Santa Claus is real." The comment came from the same voice at the back of the room. The Hun scanned the office for the culprit. Everyone there knew the chief had to justify overtime and present a balanced budget to city council. Unfortunately, the mayor's word was about as reliable as a dollar store battery. Having said his piece, the captain turned to Lieutenant Harris and told her to carry on.

"Alright people, what do we have on Delancey so far?" She eyeballed Detectives Campbell and Knudsen.

Lynda replied, "Not much, LT, I just finished the sudden death report. We're waiting on the autopsy and his wife is out of town. We have to follow up with tenants in the victim's building...many didn't answer their doors during the original canvass and some have other residences outside the city."

Harris turned to Knudsen. "Divvy up your list among the squad and track 'em down. Borrow bodies from Robbery, I'll talk to the captain. You got anything to add, Square Head?"

"Um...he wore a toupee..."

The room burst into laughter but the Hun wasn't impressed. "You're lucky the boss didn't hear that...he'd bust you down to parking detail. This is serious people...we all know how money talks, and Delancey had a shit-load of it."

Detective Scott spoke up. "I thought I should bring this to your attention, LT. He's not the only millionaire murdered in the last couple of weeks."

"Is that supposed to mean something, Hacker? Everyone knows the richer they are, the more enemies they have...probably because of all the people they shit on to get where they are. Let's worry about the mayor's golfing buddy for now. I don't need the captain taking another strip off my ass."

Abigail Brown leaned over and whispered in Ackley's ear. "With the size of her ass, she'd never miss it." Scott clamped a hand over his mouth to hold back the swig of coffee he almost spewed.

The Hun glared at Brown. "Do you have something useful to add, Crunch?"

"No, boss."

Harris did a quick about-face and almost lost her balance when the shifting bulk of one ass cheek slammed into the other. She waddled back to her office; one corner of her blazer tucked into her slacks.

Abigail and Ackley checked each other, trying not to laugh. She waved a hand over her face to wipe away the smile. "Show me what you're talking about, partner."

17
Patterns

Brown and Scott huddled behind the computer screens at his desk. She asked, "What have you found and what are you thinking?"

"Not much...but our victims Humboldt and Bulmer were both wealthy. And now we have Delancey."

"So, you *are* saying someone's knocking off the rich? I knew Bulmer was well off, but I haven't got into Humboldt's financials yet. What kind of money are we talking about?"

"Humboldt and Delancey are millionaires, Bulmer a billionaire. If that's not enough to grab your girdle...Dunn and Cummings' latest vic, Norbert Lee, is also rich and shameless."

"My girdle?"

"Sorry...it's something my gramma used to say."

Abigail was expressionless. "That's quite a coincidence, and you know how I feel about them. If you're thinking serial, the MOs are about as similar as Miami and Minneapolis. Did you check any further, or try outside the city?"

"Not yet...I wanted to run it by you or the LT first, but she doesn't seem too interested in my theory. I can't just search 'rich people killed in Michigan'. It's gonna take some finagling."

"Don't sweat it. The Hun doesn't get homicide yet. There's no quick turn around like in narcotics. See what else you can dig up before we get too excited about possible connections."

Abigail's phone rang and she went off in the direction of Lynda Campbell's desk. She wanted to lend a hand, and perhaps cherry-pick potential witnesses before the lieutenant took it upon herself to hand out assignments personally. One secret to Brown's success was jumping on a lead quickly, before those above her stuck their noses in and tried to micro-manage the case to make themselves look good.

Scott watched his former partner walk away. She was tall, slender, pretty, and smart. The kind of woman he could never have. Abigail's milk chocolate skin only made her more exotic and attractive. She was single, probably because she was more dedicated to her job than any of the other detectives. The only man she seemed to spend time with was her uncle, Bill Meyers, a retired police officer who raised her after her parents died.

The computer geek let his eyes wander around the detective office. Lynda Campbell was good-looking too, but she went for the rugged type, like the aboriginal man she followed out west. There were no other women in major case, unless you counted Jamila the Hun. He shuddered at the thought and had to wonder what her husband saw in her. Maybe she was a tiger in bed.

Ackley saw Martha Wells leaving the captain's office. Now, there was a woman he'd like to have his way with...not only in his dreams. He barely knew her, but her thoughtfulness touched him; she sent him a get-well card and some magazines when he was recovering in the hospital from his gunshot wound. He planned to follow up and say thank you when released, but he chickened out.

The detective cleared his mind of carnal thoughts and turned his attention to the search engine queued up on the center screen. Scott's gut told him there was a connection between the wealthy homicide victims. And his partner said he should always go with his gut.

18
Witnesses

Campbell and Knudsen worked the phones, trying to track down Delancey's wife. Brown scooped up a piece of paper from her friend's desk with the letterhead, Delta Pharmaceuticals. On it was a list of management staff and the name and number of the CEO's personal assistant, Helen Lipinski. Abigail pointed the name out to Lynda, who nodded her permission, and waved her off.

Brown figured it was a good place to start inquiries; at Delancey's place of business. Since the Hun let Ackley out of the office earlier, she thought about bringing him along. A quick glance in his direction revealed he was completely engrossed. She decided to leave him be so he could work his magic. She enjoyed having him as a partner and a sidekick. What he lacked in street smarts, he made up for with an abundance of raw intelligence. That would probably make him her boss someday. If there were any links or information useful to their cases in cyber space, Scott would find them.

Delta Pharmaceuticals head office was in Livonia, just off the Jeffries Freeway. A woman who Detective Brown could only describe as Mini Mouse, showed up within minutes after the front desk clerk summoned her. Abigail was a tall woman, and immediately felt self-conscious when Helen

Lipinski came around from behind the desk, and the detective found herself a full head above her.

Delancey's personal assistant suggested they talk over coffee at the new Tim Horton's, across the street. It was a Canadian franchise Brown became familiar with when she dated a man from Windsor. The two women left the front door side by side, Abigail consciously slouching to lessen the difference in height.

Lipinski insisted she buy the coffee, saying Delancey paid her well and she wanted to help in any way she could. The assistant added she was more comfortable speaking outside the office, that some questions might be sensitive or involve others within the company.

"Why would you say that, Miss...I assume it's Miss. Do you suspect foul play by someone you work with?"

"Not necessarily. It's just that...well, Mr. Delancey was very demanding and he created a competitive environment for his company executives. It was dog-eat-dog, and his two vice- presidents were vying for the top spot. The board said a CEO shouldn't be running every day operations and he needed to select a president to take over his duties."

"I'll need both their names—perhaps you can help set up appointments for me to speak with them individually. Anyone else you think might want to see your boss dead?"

"I didn't say the VPs wanted him dead but I understand your question. Nobody from here... but there are others."

"I'm sorry, I don't follow."

Lipinski blew lightly on her hot tea, and took a sip. "Lance...I mean Mr. Delancey...made quite a few enemies during his last merger. He promised to absorb the target's executives, but immediately let them go after restructuring."

"I'd like those names too, if you can get them for me?"

"Not a problem...I've already started a list in anticipation of your investigation. Lance appreciated my organizational skills and I know what you need. I'm a big fan of Law and Order."

Abigail swallowed the last bite of her oatmeal cookie and brushed the crumbs off the table with the back of her hand. She ignored the part about the television show.

"You keep calling him Lance...were the two of you close?"

"Not as close as he might like. I mean he was a big flirt, but I think he got off on playing games...with women and business associates alike; the thrill of the hunt and all that. Besides, his wife is the jealous type and had a private investigator on speed dial."

"That's interesting. How do you know that?"

"Her finances. I monitor all the Delancey's company and personal expenses...Lance didn't trust anyone, even his own accountant. He knew his wife was keeping tabs on him."

"Sounds like he trusted you?"

Lipinski finished her tea, wrapped the used bag in her napkin, and stuffed it into the empty cup. "For the most part, I believe so. I'm one of his longest-serving employees and I've always been honest with him. He seemed genuinely surprised when I told him about the PI. I really need to get back to the office. I have the employee lists and boxes of mail in my office."

"Mail?"

"Hate mail...hundreds of letters and emails from disgruntled and pissed off employees that either got passed over for promotion or let go during takeovers, mergers, and restructuring. I thought you might want those too...the TV detectives always ask for that kind of stuff."

Regardless of her taste in television, Abigail thought the woman would make a good detective, maybe better than some of her co-workers.

"Wow, Helen, I can see why Mr. Delancey kept you around. You're very efficient. I'll come back to your office and gather up that stuff."

Abigail followed the tiny woman out the door. She was happy Lipinski had supplied and gathered so much information. She was not happy about all the man-hours it would take to sift through it all.

19
Knocking

Dunn and Cummings had the tedious job of canvassing Lance Delancey's condominium building. It was one of those routine things that had to be done while investigating any serious crime. People didn't always call the police when they saw something amiss or didn't realize what they saw was suspicious. In other cases, they didn't give a damn.

A successful executive, he occupied a custom-designed penthouse, covering the entire top floor of a building he owned. The unit offered an unobstructed view of downtown Detroit, the river, and the Canadian shoreline. Apart from the main elevator accessing all floors, Delancey had a special lift put in to whisk his car up from the basement to a garage in his apartment.

With twenty units on each of the other nine floors, the detectives had their work cut out for them.

Always chomping at the bit for more action, Dunn complained to his partner. "You realize this is going to take us all day."

"It's part of the job, junior, and according to the captain we'll get paid extra if we have to work overtime. I realize you are decades from retirement, but they're gonna kick me out one day soon and I need all the extra cash I can get my hands on. Our pension is crap and I'm too old to start another career."

"Shit, partner, if you can stay awake long enough you can work as a Walmart greeter. They hire the challenged and senile."

"Ha-ha. It sucks getting old...you'll see. I'll take the lower four floors; heights make me dizzy."

Dunn scrunched his face. "That means I have an extra floor."

"You're the Olympic athlete...you can handle it."

"Yeah...yeah. Hey, hang on a sec. What about our crispy critter...are we just supposed to let that case gather dust? He's a rich dude too."

"But not the mayor's bum-buddy...besides, ours is not to reason why..."

"Don't give me that do or die macho marine bullshit...I was still in grade school when you were killing babies in the rice paddies."

20
Calling

Detective's Campbell and Knudsen worked their way through a personal telephone directory recovered from the Delancey residence. Its pink leather cover, a woman's handwriting, and names of family members, led them to believe the phone book belonged to Mrs. Deanna Delancey.

The female half of the B Team called the numbers one by one, starting with known family, trying to find Mrs. Delancey. Her partner worked the computer, googling her name and checking social media sites. It turned out the woman was a bit of a philanthropist, who sat on the boards of two charities, one local, and one in West Palm Beach, Florida.

In the interest of saving some legwork, Knudsen called WPB Police and asked for their assistance in tracking down Deanna Delancey. He spoke to a detective there, explaining how they were investigating her husband's death and as far as they knew, she hadn't been notified. The West Palm investigator assured Knudsen he would call him immediately, if and when the widow was located.

Campbell heard a familiar voice across the room and the usual profanity that came with it. Abigail Brown had forced a cart through the office door, and spilled the contents of a filing box. The veteran detective was known for her potty mouth, but Lynda thought her friend might have set a new world record for her latest string of profanity. She wasn't sure whether to laugh or go and help. Ackley Scott was already in motion, and he made it across the room quick enough to catch an armful of files before they joined the others on the floor. Although he never budged from his seat, the Square Head called out, asking if she had a license to drive that thing.

Hearing the expletive description of Abigail's mishap, the Hun popped her head out her office like a whack-a-mole. "Dump that stuff in Sleeper's corner...he and Bulldog came up empty on their canvass and are on the way back in. And don't be shy, people, y'all can feel free to dig in." Covered in flaky crumbs, Harris had a partially eaten croissant in her hand. She stuffed what was left of it into her mouth on the way back into her office.

Abigail had given her boss a heads up about the files on the way in. Scott scooped up the mess on the floor, trying to keep as many files intact as he could. He fell in behind his partner while she pushed the cart to the back of the office. On the way by Lynda's desk, Abigail paused for a second. "We need to chat. Delancey's personal assistant gave me all this and more. She's quite the little firecracker."

21
Overtime

Lynda Campbell glanced up at the wall clock and sighed. "Guess we won't be catching up with copious amounts of wine tonight."

Abigail put a hand on her friend's shoulder. "Maybe we should scoff that bottle of scotch the captain keeps in his filing cabinet, while we're stuck here sorting through files all night."

"What is all this stuff?"

"Hate mail, mostly. Delancey's assistant, Ms. Lipinski says he had a lot of enemies...from disgruntled executives, to employees who were transferred, laid off, or fired. These are their letters, emails, and even some recorded phone messages. Apparently, he was a nasty prick, who treated everyone like shit. I'm not quite sure why, but it seems the only person he trusted was his personal assistant."

"Was he banging her?"

Abigail moved the stack of files from the corner of Lynda's desk and slid her rump onto it. "I think not...according to her it was all business between them. Lipinski said she knew Mrs. Delancey had a private investigator on retainer, who monitored her husband. I guess the lack of trust went both ways in their marriage."

"Was our victim a player?"

"The assistant had her suspicions but she didn't elaborate. I firmly believe Lipinski was strictly in it for the money and didn't care what her boss did on his own time. She did admit he was a huge flirt, but she had no personal interest in the man."

Dunn and Cummings walked into the office; the junior partner three steps ahead, as usual. He froze in his tracks when he spotted the file cart parked by his desk.

"What's all this shit?"

Brown answered. "LT said to put it there...hate mail from the vic's office...she wants us to go through it and look for suspects."

"By 'we', you mean me and Cummings."

Campbell piped up. "Don't get your nuts caught in your boxers, we're in this for the long haul, and you're not alone."

Knudsen piped up. "He wears tighty-whities. I've seen him in the locker room turning them inside out to hide the skid marks."

Chuckles and snickers came from the men. The women were used to hearing such things in their male-dominated world, and ignored the comment. Abigail heard much worse in the military.

Cummings leafed through some of the stacked files. He sat down, droopy-eyed, as if he needed a nap. Lead detective on the case, Campbell walked over to their corner and offered help. "Let's sort through these together and weed out any that aren't persons of interest." She glanced back over her shoulder, signaling the others. "We can make separate piles on the table."

The team gathered in the corner and each took a handful of files back to their desks.

Lieutenant Harris came out of her office with her sweater and purse draped over her arm. "I'll check in with y'all later. Call me if you come up with anything useful." Even with six sets of eyes pushing her oversized ass out the door, it was still a tight fit.

22
Grinding

The Hun was an easy target, and bashing the boss went on for another five minutes after she left. The major case investigators spent a couple hours at their own desks before they gathered around the big table in the center of the bullpen. It was often used in such cases. There they could brainstorm the available information.

Files of persons-of-interest were stacked like a game of Jenga, with each detective adding a layer instead of removing one. Lynda asked Ackley if he could start searching the list of names she pulled from the stack.

Before he could get up and leave the table, a delivery boy dropped off a box of deli sandwiches, courtesy of Jamila the Hun. The detectives shared confused looks and shrugs, before digging in. In the way of an explanation, Dunn said Harris was like that when he worked for her in narcotics. She was unpredictable, but always had their backs and made sure her crew never went hungry. With mouths stuffed with tuna, egg salad and pastrami, appreciative nods came from all around the table. They continued browsing hate mail while they ate.

Knudsen was reaching for the last sandwich, when his cell phone rang. It was the West Palm Beach detective and he confirmed the address of the Delancey condo. He went there, questioned the doorman, and was told the wife left the night before. The Florida cop said it cost him fifty bucks to find out Deanna Delancey ordered a taxi to the Breakers Hotel, and left with an overnight bag.

Knudsen had the speaker on and glanced around the table for any other questions or input before ending the call. He commented on how expensive information was down there, and told the West Palm detective he had a steak dinner coming if he was ever in Detroit.

The group fell into a discussion, about the wife's suspected infidelity, and how they should handle notifying the woman of her husband's death. They had more questions than answers, and they still needed to interview her.

Campbell decided to run it up the chain of command, in an attempt to avoid the wrath of the mayor. She called Lieutenant Harris and relayed what they'd learned. Silence hung on the other end of the line, like a slumbering fruit bat.

"Nothin's ever simple when it comes to the rich, is it, Soup? We need to handle this with oven mitts. I gotta run it by the captain, but you've got my permission to track her ass down and tell her she needs to get home."

"Shouldn't we go down there and notify her face to face so we can gauge her reaction."

"That would be lovely, Detective, but the chief will never foot the bill, especially if he knows it's for one of the mayor's cronies. My gut says she already knows...so just say her old man is in the hospital and it's imperative she returns home. We'll pick her up at the airport. It's not really a lie since the morgue is in the hospital."

The group did more listening than reading, and all had different opinions on how to handle the woman. Scott interrupted the discussion. "Did I hear someone say the Breakers, in West Palm?"

Knudsen answered. "Yeah...the Mrs. left her condo and spent the night there. Why?"

"Interesting. Abigail, you know that PI who works for Mrs. Delancey, Mike Connors?"

"Yeah, why?"

"He has an office in Detroit, but his home address is the Breakers, in West Palm Beach."

23
Suspected

Surprise was something few seasoned homicide investigators ever experienced, but exclamations and comments from the group said otherwise. Abigail confirmed how she was told by the vic's personal assistant, that his wife had the PI on retainer, and it was his ongoing mission to watch her husband.

Lynda interjected. "Can it be that simple...a love triangle where the lover takes out the hubby so he can live happily ever after with the rich widow?"

"Sounds cut and hung out to dry to me, partner." Karl replied. "Maybe now we'll get a free trip to Florida." A huge grin split his face.

Campbell's phone rang; it was the lieutenant. "Put me on speaker, Soup, so everyone can hear me. It seems news travels at light speed in millionaire circles...the captain said Mrs. Delancey already knows about her husband's death and she'll be on the first flight home, in the morning. She and her lawyer will be in our office at 9am."

More looks of surprise came from the others gathered around the table.

"So, listen up, people. Soup...you and Square Head prep for the interview. The rest of you call it a night and I'll see you in the morning."

Brown piped up. "LT, we have information that she might be having an affair with her private investigator, who she was with..."

"I don't want to hear about that right now, it will give me nightmares. Rich people. We'll discuss it in the morning, but make sure everyone there is on the same page...I'm sure the captain will make an appearance and want an update." Frowns, nods, and some mumbling was her only response. The lieutenant hung up.

Lynda let her eyes wander around the table, checking the faces of her co-workers one by one. "There you have it, folks. We have a suspect, whether we agree or not. Ackley, can you give me a printout of what we have on Connors before you leave?"

"Sure. I haven't had a chance to get into Deanna Delancey's social media yet."

Karl Knudsen interjected. "That's okay, man, I'm already into it."

Campbell thanked everyone for their help and asked they leave her the files on any other persons of interest. She would check those for elimination purposes. Dunn had already packed up and was halfway out the door. Cummings yawned, focused on the clock. Brown thumbed through her notebook, checking the information Lipinski provided. Her twisted face said she was chewing on a thought.

Lynda saw the expression and asked, "Something bothering you, Abbs?"

"I'm not sure...Connors sounds a bit too convenient...the perfect patsy."

"Wow, that's a leap..."

"I said I wasn't sure...just a gut feeling. I'm confident you'll iron it all out tomorrow, when you talk to the black widow."

Lynda laughed. "That sounds appropriate. Thanks again for your help tonight."

"No problem...team effort...right?" She turned and headed for her desk.

Ackley went through the process of shutting his computers down. He reached out and caught Abigail's elbow on the way by. "Something doesn't smell right to you, partner?"

"We'll see...life just stinks, sometimes."

24
Saturday

The gang was all there Saturday morning, even Lieutenant Harris. She said the captain promised time in lieu for working on their day off. "Like money in the bank," she said, when trying to justify having the whole squad there.

Lance Delancey's autopsy results were waiting for Campbell and Knudsen. Cause of death was an opioid overdose, more specifically the ingestion of enough oxycodone to kill an elephant. The coroner's report said there was some alcohol, what appeared to be whiskey, in his stomach, but barely any food substance. That, and the number of opiates consumed, would explain the regurgitation.

The report also contained photographs of what appeared to be hand marks on the victim's throat, suggesting an attempt at strangulation, but the hyoid bone was intact. There was light bruising where the wrists were bound, and severe bruising in the kidney area, as if the man was punched or beaten. The victim's previous surgery scars confirmed his identity.

To help the investigation along, Dunn listed the remaining persons of interest for follow-up and elimination. Cummings booked off sick—not an unusual occurrence for the aged warrior. Scott continued to navigate cyber space for anything he could dig up on the widow and Mike Connors. Brown looked into the financials Lipinski had provided her.

Abbigail learned a lot about the deceased from his assistant's impeccable notes and files. His business dealings were quite complex and would have to be deciphered by a forensic accountant. It was abundantly clear he paid out millions in alimony and divorce settlements to his first two wives. There were no children involved. Lipinski believed there was a prenuptial agreement between Delancey and his latest wife, but there was no evidence of it or life insurance documents in the files.

Deanna Delancey and her lawyer, scheduled to be there at 9am for her interview with Campbell and Knudsen, arrived fashionably late at 9:35am. The B Team headed for the interview room. Out of curiosity, Brown joined the lieutenant behind the two-way glass to monitor the conversation. Harris was obliged to be there, so she could keep the captain apprised of the investigation, but Abigail's motive was personal curiosity.

A suspect or witness's first reaction is priceless, sometimes enough to steer the investigation in a particular direction. The seasoned homicide detective had seen her share of killers and guilty people. She also had experience in profiling, something that might help down the road if their case had to rely solely on circumstantial evidence.

Brown felt the chill from her side of the glass. Deanna Delancey's face was as chiseled and cold as an ice sculpture. She was in her late forties and attractive, but puffy lips and taught skin around her eyes said plastic surgery. Fake lashes and heavy makeup added to the effect. She was no expert, but the detective would bet money the boobs were fake too. They were entirely too large for her petite frame, and accented by a push-up bra and low neckline.

The widow answered basic tombstone questions with a simple yes or no, as her lawyer probably instructed. He did most of the talking. If the woman didn't have anything to hide, she was sure going out of her way to appear guilty. Deanna Delancey displayed no surprise or remorse at the mention of her husband's violent death.

Legal counsel went so far as to explain how Mrs. Delancey had nothing to do with her husband's business affairs, and how he had made several enemies over the years with his shrewd tactics. Knudsen attempted to throw her off guard by commenting on her nice tan and asking how the weather was in Florida. She turned to her mouthpiece, who said it wasn't unusual for his client to spend time at her condo in West Palm Beach.

Detective Campbell forced eye contact with the ice queen and asked about Mike Conners. Delancey stared past the detective at the mirrored glass and didn't even blink. As if on cue, her lawyer said Mr. Conners is Mrs. Delancey's personal bodyguard and chauffer. When asked why she spent the night at his hotel, legal counsel put his hand on his client's arm, and told the detectives she didn't have to answer that.

Before the investigators could ask anything else, he said the interview was over. Mrs. Delancey had family to notify, and a funeral to arrange for her late husband.

The partners faced each other. Campbell furled her forehead in thought. Knudsen rolled his eyes. With no response from the two detectives, the widow got up from her chair.

Campbell held up a finger and asked, "Don't you want to see your husband...to confirm it's him or at least say goodbye?"

The lawyer answered once again and said it wouldn't be necessary.

On the other side of the glass, Brown turned to Harris. "The cold-hearted bitch didn't even ask how he died."

25
Cronies

Detectives Campbell and Knudsen were discussing Delancey's interview with their lieutenant in her office, when Captain Zawadski showed up at the door. "Sorry I missed the questioning. I was tied up in a meeting with the mayor. Now that the widow is cleared, he wants to know if we have another suspect."

Lieutenant Harris gave her boss a once over. Judging by the wet bottoms of his pant legs and the golf shirt he donned, she deduced the captain's meeting took place on the links at the country club. If he was with the mayor, how the hell did they already know how the interview went. She checked her detectives' faces to see if they wondered the same thing. "I'm sorry to burst the mayor's bubble, Captain, but Mrs. Delaney hasn't been officially cleared as a suspect. After her well-rehearsed interview, we have more questions than answers."

Zawadski fiddled with loose change in his pants pocket. The skin tone of his face took on a deeper shade of rouge. "The mayor is very distraught over the loss of his close friend...their wives sit on the same charity board." The hand in his pocket formed a fist while his last words hung in the air.

"I'm just telling you what we think..."

"I don't care what you *think*, Lieutenant, it's about what you can prove. And you haven't proved to me that Deanna Delancey killed her husband."

Harris took a deep breath to hold her composure. "I never said she did it, Captain, but there's something going on between her and her private investigator. We're just getting into it. It takes time to sort these things out and to build a case."

The problem was Zawadski had no idea what it took. He should never have been put in charge of Major Case, let alone get promoted to Captain. The mayor's cronies thought the posting would look good on his resume when he applied to be chief. He spent little time on the streets, and took the administrative route through community services, and corporate development. He had zero experience as an investigator.

His face was as red as a pimple ready to burst. The captain stepped between Campbell and Knudsen and slammed a fist on Harris' desk. "If she's a viable suspect, I want to hear it from the DA. If she's not, then move the hell on and find the real killer so we can close this case." Zawadski turned and marched out of the office, looking a bit taller than when he came in.

26
Others

Jamila Harris was used to being shit on by those above her. It was the natural order of things in many organizations including the police department. There was a chain of command. The link between her captain and the chief was stretched to the breaking point. It was a balancing act for the female lieutenant, a rank normally filled by men.

Her manpower and resources weighed heavy on the mayor's side of the scale, but she also had to consider the chief's side. The top cop had already inquired about the status of the Mark Bulmer case, another wealthy victim with friends in high places. The chief got grief from Grosse Pointe's upper crust, and passed it on to Harris... a burden that came with rank.

More worried about her own ass, than the unit's clearance rate, Harris instructed Detectives Brown and Scott to continue working Bulmer. Abigail was more than happy to leave the Delancey case in her rearview mirror. She knew Campbell had her work cut out for her, dealing with the black widow and her expensive mouthpiece.

Momentum had been lost on the Bulmer case. The first forty-eight hours had long passed. It pissed her off how the affluent and powerful ranked which wealthy man was more important than the others. She agreed with fictional L.A. homicide detective Harry Bosch, whose motto was '*everybody counts or nobody counts*'. It wasn't anything new for Abigail. She experienced the same thing in Afghanistan, when generals decided which villages would get U.S. relief funds.

She waved Ackley into her office. It was quieter and they could concentrate on the case. "So, partner, have you had any time to work on your theory that someone's knocking off the rich and shameless? As much as the Ice Queen or her PI lover might look good in the Delancey case, I'm sensing something more nefarious at work here."

"You're thinking serial killer, aren't you? You know the mayor will blow a gasket if he catches wind of that."

"I'm not ready to concede this is the work of one killer...not yet. It doesn't even come close to fitting the profile. No, I think there's another connection linking these killings. Maybe its business related somehow...corporate takeovers or some other kind of big money bullshit we haven't discovered yet."

"I know you like to put everything up on your wall when putting a case together...have a look." Scott swung his lap top around so she could see the screen, and slid his chair to the side of her desk. "I've found five in the last two months...Delancey, Bulmer, Humboldt, Lee, and Albert Pearson up in Grayling...owner of a pizza chain."

"Okay, you've got my attention...anything to link them other than the fact their rich?"

"Not that I can tell so far...all different causes of death and none of their business interests appear to overlap. Detroit seems to be their only connection. They either live or work here."

Abigail leaned back in her chair, twisted her head to remove a kink in her neck. She eyed her partner and gave him a second to come clean. "Spill, Ackley, I can tell when you're holding back."

"Sorry, I went back another six months and there are five more...all wealthy and from Detroit or the surrounding areas. There's been about one killing per month. Some made the news but nobody thought much of it when you consider the murder rate and how they all died differently."

The tiny hairs on Brown's arms stood at attention. She leaned in to take a closer look. "Fuck me...and all different causes of death?"

"Yep...no two the same. Even I know serial killers have routines and rituals." He stared at his partner and shook his head. "This is way out of my league. You're the profiler...any of it make sense to you?"

Brown slumped in her chair, palmed her face with both hands, and blew air through her fingers. "Make sense of what...how rich men are being knocked off for no apparent reason, other than their financial status? Shit. Maybe there's a murder club out there and they prey on the wealthy for the fun of it. If money's a motive, how are they profiting...some kind of extortion ring?"

"Should we bring the LT in on this?"

Abigail chewed on it for a minute. "Not yet. Harris will be obligated to run it up the flag pole, and the chief and the mayor will go ape shit." She paused in thought again. "No, let's work with what we've got on Bulmer. I want to take another look at Humboldt too. There has to be common ground somewhere."

Scott nodded along in agreement.

"Can you put everything in chart form and list all the property found on each victim? One thing is bothering me...remember the numbers on the boat you thought were GPS coordinates?"

"Yeah, I've come up empty. Why?"

"The pills at Delancey's...Lynda said they were laid out on a table to form the number 849. Maybe that doesn't mean shit, but we need to check the others. Humboldt had a roll of quarters in his pocket...strange, but explainable? Forty coins...any of these numbers mean anything to you?"

Ackley shrugged and shook his head. "Beats me...wait a second...when I read over the Pearson case, the detective made mention of carving on the victim's rifle, which was also the murder weapon. His initials and the number 547 were carved into the wooden stock. The investigator was keen enough to notice the numbers were fresh in comparison to the letters."

"What the fuck? Definitely interesting, but about as useful as a screen door on a submarine. I'll talk with Dunn to see if he or Cummings found any numbers in their crispy critter's property. Can't imagine anything worthwhile that wasn't burned in the fire, but what the hell. If we're betting on this theory, we might as well go all in."

Before she could ask, Scott said he'd search the other cases for property and any notations about strange numbers. "What's next for Bulmer...any persons of interest or suspects for us to track down?"

"Good question, but I'm short on answers and weirded out by all this shit."

27
Alibis

About twenty-four hours after Deanna Delancey's interview, Mike Connors showed up at the cop shop and asked to see the detectives handling her deceased husband's case. Lieutenant Harris fetched the private investigator from the main lobby, and explained the officers in charge of the case were out speaking to witnesses. Conners shrugged and said he'd be happy to wait.

In an attempt to keep the man under wraps, she gave him a guest pass and invited him upstairs to wait in the crime unit's lobby. It was more comfortable and he could get a coffee, if so inclined. Conveniently, the waiting room was under video surveillance, and Harris had a monitor in her office.

She called Detective Campbell and told her Conners showed up on his own, and she, and her partner should come in to question him.

"Did he bring a lawyer?"

"No. But...get this...we chatted on the way up in the elevator. He's a retired Michigan State Trooper. I don't know what it is about cops, but they never ask for a lawyer...as if they know the law and can protect themselves, I guess. I'll track down the Bulldog and see what else he has on the PI. I will leave everything on your desk so you can study up before you interview him."

"A retired cop, huh, this ought to be interesting. We'll be there in twenty."

Knudsen only heard bits of the phone conversation. "Who's a retired cop?"

"The widow Delancey's private investigator...he was with the state police."

"No shit. He's come in on his own without a lawyer...typical state cop, confident and cocky."

"Can you call the office and see if Dunn's in, he was supposed to get the 411 on Connors. It'd be nice to be well-prepared before we talk to him."

Knudsen thumbed the buttons on his phone. "Damn, nobody's answering. I'll try his cell.

When the B Team arrived at their office, Ackley Scott was the only one there. He pointed to Campbell's desk and said Dunn left them everything he could find on the PI. Lynda put her purse down. "Where's the LT?"

"She figured you'd be in shortly and put your guy in the box to see how he'd react being alone on the opposite side of an interrogation table. She's watching from the viewing room."

Knudsen skimmed Dunn's file on Connors. "There's a note in here from the West Palm cop. It says our boy is mostly a sneak and peak private dick...tries to catch cheating spouses in the act. Loyal to his clients, according to them...won't give up his sources but did help the police there with a high-end jewelry heist."

Campbell raised her brow. "No dirt?"

"Nothing I see here."

"Alright...let's have at him. You take the lead. You're more prepared and I'll watch for tells and body language."

They met Lieutenant Harris in the viewing room. She was fixated on Connors, no more than ten feet from her, on the opposite side of the glass. The Hun turned to her detectives when they entered the room. "Cool as the other side of a pillow. He came prepared...see the file in front of him. This guy knows how to stickhandle so keep the puck away from him. Remember it's your interview, you ask the questions, and you control the pace."

Campbell and Knudsen turned and headed out the door. "Good luck, Detectives."

If the Connors interview took place on the Bonneville Salt Flats, the trio could have set a land speed record. The retired trooper turned private investigator, sat there quietly while the detectives introduced themselves and explained why they wanted to question him. They asked their first pointed question. He simply smiled and pushed his file folder across the table.

Campbell flipped open the folder to examine its contents. Knudsen asked another question, but Connors remained silent and tilted his head toward the file. He ignored the next question, folded his hands on the table, and watched Campbell. She slid the file to her partner.

The first page in the file read like an official police report. It was a chronology of his whereabouts and movements for the previous five days, which included the day of Delancey's murder. The next page was a list of receipts, with copies attached, proving where Connors stayed, slept, ate, bought groceries, and got gas for his car.

Campbell turned to the mirrored glass which Harris was standing behind.

Knudsen tried questioning the suspect about some of the receipts but Connors only shrugged and said, "Everything you need is in that file, Detective."

The investigators looked at each other. The lieutenant knocked on the window, signaling their interview was over before it really got started.

28
Bulmer

Abigail let her partner work his magic in data land. She leafed through her inbox and set aside any reports received on the Mark Bulmer case. There was a notification from their crime lab. Epithelial skin cells collected from the crime scene were sent away for analysis. The seasoned detective went into the case files on her computer and brought up the forensics report.

According to the specialist who examined the boat, traces of skin were found on the nylon rope attached to the life buoy. He went on to say glove marks were found below deck. The evidence collected from the rope was probably from a bare forearm. The killer may have a visible rope burn.

Brown was impressed. Initially, she didn't think much of the small-town investigators, but their forensics specialist seemed more than capable. DNA was a tricky thing, and not always extractable from skin. Even if the extraction was successful, the sample had to match a known offender in the data bank to be of any use.

It was the crime scene technician's opinion the prints, blood, and all other DNA evidence belonged to the victim. A supplementary report attached to the file, confirmed the victim's prints and blood type. Abigail made a note to call the crime lab herself, and ask them to rush their examination of the skin cells.

The detective scanned crime scene photos. She took them herself to get a better idea of the collection of evidence. Educating herself enabled her to discuss it later with forensic scientists. Examining a photograph of the yellow nylon rope, she formed an image in her mind, of how the killer's forearm could have scraped it.

Abigail scrolled though the remaining photos, hoping something else might catch her eye. She knew the chance of solving the case on a solitary DNA sample was like trying to win the lottery. None of the other images piqued her interest. Since it was a joint investigation with Grosse Pointe, she read all of their reports.

The statement from Mrs. Bulmer didn't offer anything that might incriminate anyone. They were happily married, but her husband was a workaholic and didn't spend much time at home. His boat was a sore point for her, since he bought it knowing she was terrified of the water. She never set foot on it. She couldn't think of anyone who might want to harm her husband, but he was a corporate raider, who took over smaller companies, making some people very unhappy along the way. She added how her husband believed in rewarding good work, and generously gave to those loyal to him.

Abigail made notes to check with Grosse Pointe investigators, Bulmer's work place, and some victims of his recent take-overs. She paused for a moment and stared at Ackley. Only the top of his head was visible above his computer screens.

She considered the serial angle they talked about and wondered if it made any sense. It did not.

29
Justice

Surprise! Joel Humboldt's murder made the newspaper. Most people will think it was just another mugging in a dark alley; a crackhead looking for quick cash to buy his next rock. The reporter made the victim out to be someone important, just because he owned a bunch of muffler shops. Why do the rich get all the press?

Pearson died in the heat of the moment, but I planned Humboldt's murder better. Too bad, things don't always go according to Hoyle. I didn't know exactly where the muffler man would die. I hadn't decided yet. Opportunity knocked when I saw him leave the hotel and walk into the alley across the street. Why didn't the privileged asshole simply smoke out front of the hotel like other guests? Maybe he didn't want his wife to see him indulging in the dirty habit, or the ass told her he quit.

Seeing that wealthy bastard walk into a dark alley was too good to be true. My mind raced while Humboldt pulled a pack of cigarettes from his pocket. Cloaked in darkness, only the lighter's flame and exhaled smoke gave his position away. I needed a quick plan and a silent weapon. From the glove box, I grabbed the Swiss Army knife my father gave me on my twelfth birthday.

Checking the mirrors to see if anyone else was around, I caught my reflection. I missed my dad; I can never forget watching him wither and die. Mom moved to Arizona to live with her sister the year before that. I haven't spoken to her since.

Parked in the hotel lot, I had a clear view of the hotel's front entrance and the mouth of the alley across the street. When Humboldt stepped into the dark the decision to take action was easy. With my trusted pocketknife in hand, I thought about how I would kill Joel Humboldt. There was no reason to show mercy...should it be quick or should the asshole suffer? I found the longest blade and examined it. Used right it could cause enough damage to kill. Checking for any vehicle or pedestrian traffic, I exited the car, crossed the street, and slipped into the shadows.

It is like replaying a favorite movie in my head. I remember every step I took approaching that alley. Humboldt was only a few feet from the sidewalk, barely visible in the low light. The glow from the cigarette lit his face as he took a last drag and discarded the butt.

I startled him. The coward took a step back, snapping his head from side to side, looking for a path of escape. I stuck him with the blade before he could turn to run. He hesitated at the sudden pain, but put-up little resistance. I delivered more knife thrusts into his chest and abdomen. He tried to call out but pain and surprise stole his breath. The muffler man staggered backwards, slipping further into the alley.

Uncontrollable rage took over...I kept stabbing the man. When his legs gave out, he landed on his ass. Humboldt used his hands, trying to pull himself backwards, his heels dragging on the pavement. Then, as if his feet snagged on something, he fell onto his back and gasped for air until his breathing stopped.

It wasn't a perfect murder, and again I rushed my decision to kill, but it had to be done. I will get better at it. I probably should have checked for a pulse to make sure Humboldt was dead, but it all worked out. Once again, I'm sure I left no evidence and no witnesses. There wasn't a soul on the street when I returned to my car.

Killing again bothered me a lot less than I thought it would. There were no feelings of guilt or remorse, only a sense of satisfaction. My quest for justice is only beginning. The first kills weren't even responsible for my mother leaving or my father's death, but they're all the same. These men are rich and powerful, but still vulnerable. Their egos and arrogance keep them from hiring bodyguards or private security to ensure their safety...lucky me.

Although I sometimes find them too easy, I love doing the daily Sudoku and crossword puzzles in the paper...they give me a sense of pride and accomplishment. But I still feel a deep yearning inside, like an itch I can't scratch. I think it's because my mission isn't finished.

More need to die.

30
Mattering

Lynda Campbell slinked into Abigail's office and plopped into the chair in front of her desk. She sighed deeply to make sure she had her friend's attention.

Deep in thought but interrupted, Brown looked over her computer screen. "What's up Lynn?"

"A whole lotta nothing. We're getting nowhere on the Delancey case...the wife and her lover, have come up clean. My gut tells me they were up to something but I can't prove any of it...the spouse is usually suspect number one and money is a prime motive, right? Not that we have any proof of those theories. The PI looked good but his alibi's tighter than a nun's petunia."

Abigail laughed. "Good one...sounds like something I'd say."

Lynda shrugged. "I know, hey? You're rubbing off on me. I heard the Hun put you back on the Bulmer case...the guy who got dragged behind his own boat?"

Abigail closed her laptop and interlaced her fingers on top of it. "Yup, but not before he was shot with his own spear gun."

"What? Overkill, don't you think? Any good leads? I know you got pulled away for my case. Sorry."

"No sweat. It seems the rich and powerful decide which cases we need to investigate. It sucks to lose momentum but nothing really came to light in the first forty-eight anyway." She paused in thought, deciding if she should tell Lynda about the theory she and Ackley were working on. "Maybe we should take advantage of the lull and do that girls' night we talked about."

"For sure. That's another reason I popped in...a girlfriend cancelled tomorrow night...do you remember the psychic your friend Norm told us about? The four of us were going to make a night of it?"

"Vaguely...Lebanese guy?"

Lynda leaned forward, putting her palms on Abigail's desk. Her voice went up an octave. "Yeah. I found his phone number when I cleaned out an old purse and I made an appointment for Sherry and I tomorrow night. You wanna go? It'd be fun."

Abigail rolled her eyes. "I dunno...you believe in that stuff?"

"I didn't, until Norm talked about his sister's experience...how the guy didn't know her and mentioned things he could never have guessed."

"So, what's he gonna tell us...stuff about our non-existent love lives and how someday we'll get swept away by a knight in shining armor?

"You never know...c'mon, we can go to that little Italian restaurant near the casino and have some drinks first..."

"Oh, you mean the place behind the strip club the boys took us to? You seemed to enjoy that." Abigail clucked.

Lynda's faced flushed and she covered it with her hands. "I'm glad I don't remember much of that."

"How could you forget another woman grinding her ass in your lap?"

"I guess I blocked it out...like a traumatic event in my life." She offered a shy smile. "So, are you in? I still have a time slot reserved with Simon...his name means to listen or hear. Freaky, hey? I looked it up."

"Alright, I'll go—but only if we can have some wine first. Something tells me I'm going to need a sense of humor if someone's going to read my fortune." Abigail stared past Lynda, at the lieutenant, who was staring back at her from the bullpen. "Give me the details tomorrow...the Hun's giving me the stink-eye. She must have heard us giggling."

Lynda grabbed a file from Abigail's desk, stood up and handed it back to her. She turned and casually left the office without making eye contact with her boss, like a kid told to leave class for being disruptive. Getting back to work, Abigail opened her laptop and shook her head. There were times when she felt that Jamila the Hun truly was a descendant of the fearsome Mongolian leader.

31
Simon

Abigail thought it might be a good idea, a distraction from work, and a well-deserved girls' night out. They had a glass of wine at her place. From her downtown apartment, it was a short drive across the river, to Canada. They chatted on the way. Lynda explained how Simon usually made house calls but he didn't want to cross the border.

Abigail cracked, "Why, is he on the terrorist watch list?"

"No...I guess he's quite shy and doesn't venture too far from home. My girlfriend said she heard of him. He's not like one of those phony card readers or fortune tellers who use a crystal ball and try to conjure up ghosts from the past."

"That's too bad...there's a few ghosts I'd like to check in on."

Lynda exited the tunnel and circled the blocks north of it, trying to find the restaurant. They drove by Windsor Police Headquarters. Abigail gazed out the passenger window. "Do you think about him at all?"

"Who...Norm? Not really...well, that's a lie. I've dated since but nothing serious. We had fun but it just wasn't meant to be; trains on parallel tracks heading in opposite directions."

"I hear you, girlfriend, I'm on your train. Men, hey? Can't live with 'em but can't have great sex without them."

"He drunk-texted me a while back and I had a sex dream about him that night...woke myself up when I arched my back. The man knew what he was doing down there."

Lynda's eyes popped and they laughed. Abigail pointed to the restaurant and Lynda found a vacant parking meter on the street. She said, "La Guardia...no wonder we couldn't find it...it's smaller than I remember. I think I had pasta when we came with the guys. Did you call him back?"

"Almost, in a weak moment, when I thought about the dream. He was on a bike trip, and I just let it go. Besides, we were already into this serial shit."

Being a weeknight, the hostess seated the ladies without a reservation. Lynda told Abigail to go ahead and order the wine, and she would split the bottle with her. "At least you learned a bit about vino when you dated Norm...did he ever become a sommelier?"

"I don't believe so. He said the classes interfered with his travel agenda. The last time I talked to him he was off to South America."

"Sounds exotic and fun..."

"Maybe in another life." She ordered the Ripasso Valpolicella, a medium bodied Italian red to pair with Lynda's spaghetti bolognaise and her veal dish. They sipped wine, enjoyed their meals, and talked about everything except work.

Lynda checked her watch. "Do you need dessert? We really should get going to make our appointment with Simon. He's about twenty minutes away."

"It's Windsor...nothing's more than twenty minutes away."

Simon's house was in a Windsor subdivision. He was standing in the front door waiting for them when they pulled into his driveway. Abigail chuckled, "Guess he doesn't need a clock to know when someone's coming, hey?"

"It'll be fun...you'll see. Maybe he can help solve one of your cases."

They met Simon at his door and introduced themselves by their first names only—that was all he asked for. How much could be discovered without a surname? Simon was a short and slim man, with a receding hairline and facial creases that put him in his mid-fifties, give or take. He wore grey dress slacks, and an open-collared off-white dress shirt, partially covered by what appeared to be a homemade wool vest. He offered his hand to both women.

Abigail thought it felt like a soft dry sponge.

He was a low talker whose voice was barely louder than a whisper, and he enunciated his words to cover his European accent. Less than a minute into his spiel about what the women could expect, Lynda volunteered to go first. Simon told Abigail to make herself comfortable in the living room, and he would be back for her in about forty-five minutes. He left the room with Lynda in tow.

The house was quieter than a public library. Abigail scanned the room before taking a seat on the sofa. It looked like it was original to the house, but showed no signs of wear. Everything was neat and comfortable, but the aged décor screamed makeover. A ticking grandfather clock was the closest thing to music. There was no visible television. An intricate lace doily covered the coffee table. Placed perfectly in the middle, were two glasses of water and plate of what had to be homemade chocolate chip cookies. She couldn't resist. Abigail took in the room while the fresh goodie melted in her mouth.

There were family photos—one of Simon and a woman who appeared to be his wife, but no pictures of any children. There were women's touches throughout the room, but no other sign that anyone else lived with the man. Abigail had another cookie in her mouth before she realized what she was doing. Eating them was like smoking crack cocaine.

She took a sip of water and strained to hear anything from Lynda and Simon. On two occasions it sounded like Lynda gasped or groaned, but she didn't hear a peep from Simon. When Abigail heard their voices in the hall, she couldn't believe forty-five minutes had passed and checked the clock to confirm.

Lynda wore mixed expressions; her wide eyes and raised brow revealed shock and possibly concern, while a crooked smile said she was confused and content at the same time. She locked eyes with Abigail and mouthed the word 'wow'. Simon waited at the hall entrance and Lynda took her friend's spot on the couch. She reached for a cookie.

The quiet man led Abigail to a room at the end of the hall. A converted bedroom was the sitting room or office; sparsely furnished with a daybed, desk, and modest bookshelves lined with an assortment of leather antique-looking books. A manual typewriter sat perfectly in the center of the desk. A framed photo of a woman Simon's age sat beside it.

He told Abigail to sit wherever she would be most comfortable. She chose the desk chair. He sat on the daybed and briefly explained what he was about to do and how certain images came to him. She could ask questions but he would only describe what he saw. The homicide cop was skeptical of the whole thing, but impressed he didn't ask her any revealing questions.

It was eerie from the start. Simon broke eye contact and stared at a spot on the floor between his feet. Without hesitation, he began to describe the images he saw.

Abigail wasn't sure why but she was tense and a bit nervous, as if she just committed a crime and was being interrogated. That wasn't the case since the man spoke but asked nothing of her.

Simon said he saw her and a large man of color in a huge arena or stadium. There was a tiger. He saw another man in uniform, carrying a gun. It wasn't the same man, although the two appeared as though they might be related. Then he saw her with yet another man, younger and gravely injured. Simon paused and looked up at Abigail to see if he should go on; he didn't like to deliver negative or bad news.

She nodded for him to proceed.

Returning his gaze to the carpet, he said there was blood, and death. His body stiffened and he clasped a hand on the side of his neck. It was as if he felt pain there. He took two deep breaths to calm himself. Simon saw a goateed man riding a motorcycle on a curvy highway in the mountains.

Abigail felt goosebumps. The little old Lebanese man had referred to all of the important men in her life. How could he know these things? She held her poker face and never made a sound, amazed how he never made eye contact to gage her reaction.

Simon continued but appeared uneasy again.

She told him it was okay to go on.

He saw her in a cold room with stainless steel furniture, where strangers hovered over her. Their images appeared troubled, and were transparent or ghostlike. He grimaced, as if feeling their torment. There was another man—a stranger —his face hidden behind a newspaper. The psychic held his palms out and began to count his fingers. He saw money and numbers... random numbers.

Abigail thought he was done.

Simon lifted his head, made eye contact, and mimicked her. He fluttered his fingers, as if typing. Then he pressed his palms together and interlaced his fingers, leaving the two indexes extended, and pointing. It was the shape of a gun.

32
List

Ackley Scott didn't have much of a life outside the police department. A marriage to his therapist only lasted six months and he had no siblings. His parents lived in Florida year-round. That was good in a couple ways. First, they were too far away for surprise visits to check up on him. Second, he was able to take over their downtown apartment, paying just enough rent to cover taxes and condo fees.

The young detective enjoyed the convenience of living in the city. He was close enough to walk to work in good weather, and didn't mind using public transportation to get around. There was a People Mover station only a block from his residence. It's not that Ackley didn't like to drive. He sorely missed his old Saab. It conked out shortly after him being shot.

Living in a high security building offered him a feeling of safety. His telephone hardline allowed him access to the department's computer server. Ackley was one of only a handful of police employees allowed such a privilege. Being responsible for improving the DPD's firewall and online presence may have had something to do with the perk.

When he wasn't watching Jeopardy or competing with Justin online, trying to solve complex puzzles, Ackley worked on his police files. Although he wasn't connected to any state or federal databases, he could access any of the Major Crimes active cases. As one who liked organization, was borderline obsessive compulsive, he strived to be one-step ahead of his idol, Abigail Brown. Since he couldn't work the streets with her, he made sure she had everything at her fingertips. She was more than capable of doing the computer work herself, but more valuable working the street.

Ackley opened his laptop and pulled up the list he put together. They were wealthy victims he discovered; all publicly considered millionaires.

> Albert Pearson - Gunshot - Grayling - #547
> Joel Humboldt - Stabbing - Greek Town - #40??
> Mark Bulmer - Speared & Drowned - Grosse Pte - #3085
> Norbert Lee -Burned - Detroit - #2333
> Lance Delancey - Overdose - Highland Park - #849
> Jerome Baylor - Poisoned - Dearborn
> Winifred Nichols - High-rise Fall - Ann Arbor
> John Thomas - Electrocuted - Farmington Hills
> Brian Coulter - Strangled - Royal Oak
> Kelly O'Reilly - Hit & Run - Corktown

Ackley read the reports submitted by Dunn and Cummings on the Norbert Lee case and noted they seized the rear license plate from the burnt vehicle. The Michigan tag bore the letters and numbers 'LEE 2333'. The plate was a fake and had gone unnoticed at first.

The arson investigator took a closer look, wondering why it wasn't heavily damaged by the fire and heat. He discovered it was crafted from a heavier gage metal than the ones issued by the state. Further investigation showed 'LEE

1958' registered to that vehicle; Lee's surname and year of birth. Someone switched the car's license plate.

Ackley looked past his laptop to his desktop monitor, where he was doing Google searches on the older victims on his list. There were no unexplained numbers found in their respective sudden death reports. He would have to follow-up with the investigators. His main focus was trying to find a link between the victims, other than their financial status. There had to be something more, there always was.

He sat back in his chair and massaged his eyes. Even his fingers were sore from pounding the keyboards all evening. It was midnight and time to pack it in for the day. Ackley knew if he didn't force himself into the bedroom and get some sleep, he'd be useless at work in the morning. He got back on his laptop and sent the updated hit list to Abigail's work email.

33
Men

Abigail looked as if she was told extraterrestrials worked within the DPD. She walked into the living room and made contact with Lynda's inquiring eyes. Brown was speechless and headed for the front door. Lynda handed the psychic a hundred dollars, thanked him for the insights, and hurried to catch up with her friend.

Once in the car, she asked Abigail how it went but she couldn't wait for the answer. Lynda spilled her guts about everything that Simon told her.

"It was unbelievable, Abs...he said things about my lawyer friend, Two Snakes and my father...it blew me away. He even got up and limped around the room, like my dad does when he walks. Sorry I didn't let you answer. I'm so jacked. Of course, I was skeptical before we went but not now. How the hell does he do that?"

Abigail only stared out the windshield, her brain in high gear trying to process everything Simon said to her. She scanned the information for non-truths but there weren't any. It was too accurate to be educated guesswork.

"Abs...are you alright? You look like you saw a ghost?"

Wide-eyed and still shell-shocked, she turned to Lynda. "I might as well have."

"Why, what did he say?"

Abigail replayed Simon's words in her head at high speed, some of his visions were confusing, but they screamed for attention. Dead people, a newspaper man, numbers. She wondered how much to reveal to her friend. It would all come out eventually but she was short with her answer. "He talked about the men in my life...it was all about the men."

"Me too! How weird is that? Does that mean we don't have a life of our own?"

"Maybe. Let's get back to our side of the border...I need a drink."

Lynda continued to talk about her experience with Simon and how he could never have known about any of the images he saw.

Abigail remained consumed by her own thoughts. They exited the international tunnel and stopped at The Old Shillelagh, in Greektown. Lynda was still babbling on about all the men in her life.

After a shot of Jameson's and chasing it with half a glass of beer, Abigail interrupted her. "Sorry if I seem out of it, but Simon took me back to places I've tried to forget about, and some things I'm involved in now. I'm trying to make sense of it all."

"And here I'm doing all the talking and not listening. What's going on?"

Abigail took in another mouthful of beer. "Okay...hang on to your chair. He saw my men too...like Uncle Bill, my father, Dwayne and Norm. But he also described things that are happening now...cases at work."

Lynda didn't respond. She leaned in closer to listen.

"Promise you'll keep this to yourself until I take it up the chain of command...it's about the murders we're investigating right now. Ackley and I have a theory."

"You know you can trust me. How could Simon know about work stuff? Very little has been in the news."

"No shit...it's totally fucking weird. I think he can see dead people, and gets vibes or something from us about others we know. It doesn't make any sense to me. He saw Norm on his bike and even Dwayne when he got shot in the neck and died. And he talked about freaky shit...like me in the morgue with spirits or ghosts hovering over me."

Lynda finished her glass of beer in two gulps. "Holy crap, I don't..."

"Hang on...it gets better. I think he can see our killer, the man who's murdering the millionaires."

"What do you mean, 'our killer'? Are you saying the cases are related somehow?"

Abigail stared right through Lynda. "Yes...and not just ours...Ackley found ten murders so far...all millionaires from the Detroit area. The cause of death is different in each case."

"Someone's killing the wealthy? What links them together...what's the motive...money?"

"We can't say yet, but there's the random numbers at the recent crime scenes."

Lynda regarded her friend as if she was speaking a foreign language. "Huh? I don't follow."

"The number of pills spelled out on Delancey's table, a number carved on the murder weapon in Grayling, a number found on Bulmer's boat. Scott is checking for any strange numbers in Lee's murder, and we found a roll of quarters in Humboldt's pocket...we're not sure about those yet. I think they're all clues and we have a serial killer on our hands."

"What? Does that make any sense to you? You're the profiler."

Abigail finished her beer and signaled the bartender for two more.

"Yes and no. At this stage, I don't know enough about the killer to say if he fits the stereotype, but murdering the rich creates the pattern. We have no idea how else they might be connected or what significance the numbers have, but many serial killers have an ulterior motive and sometimes leave clues to justify their actions."

"And you haven't told the lieutenant or captain yet? What's your plan?"

"I'm still working on it but we'll have to bring them up to speed so we can pool our resources and try to link the cases. Do you have any other suspects for Delancey I'm not aware of?"

Lynda paused while the waitress put two fresh beers on the table. "We've got squat...thought for sure the wife and her lover did it, and it was all about the money...setting herself up before the marriage went south."

"I have to check in with Ackley in the morning, to see what else he's dug up. Then we'll take it to the Hun and watch her squirm in her chair while trying to figure a way to tell the captain he's got a serial killer on the loose."

"You mean jiggle in her chair..." Their laughter broke the tension.

Clinking glasses, Abigail toasted, "Here's to serial for breakfast."

34
Images

After looking at her alarm clock for what seemed like the seventeenth time, Abigail decided to get an early start to her day. Her brain replayed the evening's events repeatedly, trying to make sense of it all. How could the quiet little Lebanese man from Windsor know such things about her life? He said they presented themselves as images in his head. What exactly did that mean?

Relieving her bladder of the previous night's beer, Abigail caught her profile in the mirror. Her hair was barely mussed. She laid on her back most of the night, awake. She stood up and faced her reflection. Not bad for the big 4-O, she thought. Small lines, barely visible, creased her temples. Nobody needed to know that she dyed her hair.

Abigail went into the kitchen and poured a glass of cold water. She slid open the balcony door to check the weather. A cool breeze found its way under her Lions jersey; number 20, worn by Barry Sanders, one of Detroit's all-time greats. She was not a big football fan. Norm Strom took her to a game and bought her the shirt. She thought about the retired Windsor cop for a moment, wondering why Simon mentioned him.

Simon...he would be in her thoughts all day. She had to figure it all out. She had to know. Abigail returned to her bathroom and pulled off the jersey. The mirror called to her again. She had an athletic frame, but gravity was starting to affect certain parts of her body, important parts. Doing a full three-sixty gave her some satisfaction...it could be worse. She was told once she had the ass of a sixteen-year-old. Still, she wasn't happy with her upper body musculature. Running kept her toned, but she needed to incorporate more weight training in her workouts. Abigail pulled on an old army sweatshirt over her Lululemon body suit and slipped into her cross trainers. She did a bit of stretching to loosen up.

It was early dawn when she hit the pavement outside her front door. The one-time basketball and track star headed for the river. The city had worked hard to expand its paths, parks, and greenway along the waterfront, perhaps attempting to mirror the Canadian coastline across the river. It was a great place to run, taking in the scenery and fresh air. Red and burnt orange ripples on the water's surface reflected colors of the morning sky.

The run normally helped to clear her mind, allowing her to concentrate, and plan the day ahead. Today the river brought back images of dead women and body parts, reminders of Henry Jensen, the last serial killer she took down. Are those the images Simon referenced? Was he talking about the new murders? Tortured souls and ghosts, she was confused. Dead people. Abigail shook her head to clear the images.

Was that all there was to her life—murder and dead bodies? She liked her job for the most part, but there had to be more. Norm told her she needed to travel more, to see the world, but she was too busy with work and too young to retire. Maybe she should consider a security or consulting job. No. That wasn't for her.

The mysterious numbers were bouncing around in her head when she reached the halfway point of her run and turned back toward home. She wondered if Ackley found anything else useful. He may not have been a great street cop, but he was a good investigator, and she was grateful to have him.

Abigail picked up the pace. She aimed for a quicker time on the return trip, and liked to go full out for the last hundred yards. It stole her breath but the pump felt great.

35
Tales

Almost always the first one in the office, Abigail was surprised to see Ackley Scott. Before she settled at her desk, Lynda Campbell appeared in her doorway. "How'd you sleep last night, Abbs? I tossed and turned all night thinking about everything Simon said to me, and what he told you."

Ackley slipped past Lynda and took the chair in front of Abigail's desk. "Who's Simon?"

The two women looked at each other but didn't respond. Abigail turned to Ackley. "You're in early...did you find anything we can call a lead?"

He tilted his head toward Campbell before answering.

Abigail continued. "It's all good...I filled her in last night. I want to brief the lieutenant when she comes in...and the captain too. They need to know our thinking and what we're up against."

Lynda nodded. "Okay, let me grab my notes from my desk and we can go over your plan before the bosses get here."

Abigail organized her desk while Ackley fingered the keyboard on his laptop. "I did a bit of work last night, on 'our list'.

"And?"

"Another number...from the crispy critter case, Norbert Lee. Seems the killer swapped his vanity license plate for a fake, LEE 2333. The original tag displayed his birth year, 1958."

"For fuck's sake, I don't suppose there's anything in the reports telling us what the hell 2333 means?"

"Nope. I made printouts of the list for you and the LT. I know how you like to post these things on your wall. I used a larger font...sorry, but I noticed you seem to need longer arms to read things now. Maybe you're ready for glasses?" He pulled her copy from a folder and handed it across the desk."

Abigail browsed the list once, pulling the paper closer. "Asshole...it's that obvious?" She got up and pinned it on her corkboard, and considered the victims, their causes of death, and the mystery numbers. "I'll be damned if I can figure it out. If this is a serial, the killer is in a whole new category. I'll reach out to my instructor at Quantico and see if he's ever come across anything like this."

Scott nodded and continued to tap away on his laptop. "I'll let you get your thoughts in order. Just give me a holler when you're ready to tell the LT." He closed his computer and left her office.

Abigail fell into a trance. She stood and stared at the list as if it was a complex algebraic problem requiring a solution in order to save the world. Simon's images flashed through her mind. Returning to her desk, she checked her phone messages. The only important call was from her forensics pal, Skel, who said he lifted partial prints from some of the quarters in Humboldt's roll, but nothing suitable to submit for a match.

Brown wrote herself a note to have a closer look at the quarters. She made another note to call the DNA lab and see how they made out with the epithelial cells from the rope in the Bulmer case. With no witnesses or other viable leads, she hoped forensics could give her something to go on. The brass would want to know every resource was being used to its full potential, and that she was conducting an exhaustive investigation.

Hearing voices in the bullpen, Abigail saw Dunn holding the office door open for Lieutenant Harris. The expression on his face said it all. The orange and brown pantsuit had to be from her favorite store, Sally Ann. The stripes struggled to follow her expansive curves. Brown smiled, keeping any fashion thoughts to herself.

She decided to wait for Knudsen, Cummings and the captain. The big boss had to be brought up to speed whether she liked it or not. As the acting commander, Captain Zawadski was in charge of the entire investigation branch. Briefing everyone at once meant less repetition later.

Abigail made the call and asked the lieutenant if she could brief her, the captain, and the troops, once everyone was in. As expected, the Hun asked what the meeting concerned. Brown told her she and Scott had new information pertaining to their current murder investigations. Before Harris could question her more, she said it would be best to explain it to everyone at the same time.

Less than an hour later, the whole unit gathered in the captain's office. There was a semi-circular table facing his desk. It was large enough to seat them all. The room was set up like a theater, with Zawadski on stage in front of his audience. He thought it was great for meetings with subordinates where he would be the focus of their attention. Everyone attended except for Cummings who was off sick again. All eyes averted to the white board Detective Brown rolled into the room. On it was the list of wealthy victims she and Scott put together. The silence sat like a stagnant pond, while they all contemplated the names of the dead.

Zawadski's raspy voice cracked. "Okay, Detective...I recognize some of the names from our active cases, but what is the meaning of this list? Are we supposed to see a connection between them?"

She waved her hand over the board for effect. "It's what you don't see here, sir. We have other open cases, of course, but every name on this list is one of Detroit's elites." Brown let that sink in for a moment. "They are rich; millionaires and even billionaires."

The captain thought about the ramifications of such a profound statement.

Lieutenant Harris cut in. "You have our attention, Crunch...are you trying to tell us all the names on that list were murdered because they are wealthy?"

"It would seem that way, but we don't..."

Zawadski cut in. "But..." He hesitated; his twisted face showed the agony of a boxer hit below the belt. "But I just told the mayor we were making progress on the Delancey case...that the wife and her lover were good suspects and we're waiting on forensics for confirmation."

The lieutenant addressed her boss. "I sent you an update on that case, Captain...how your suspects had iron-clad alibis...that investigation stalled."

The captain opened his mouth to respond but turned to Brown instead. "This better be good, Detective. Please tell me how and why all these men...and one woman, have come to be on this list. Is there some kind of profile mumbo jumbo you picked up in Quantico justifying this outlandish conclusion?"

"Yes and no, sir." Abigail considered her delivery, hoping she would be convincing enough to get them all on board. "Detective Scott and I gave this careful thought, even before considering the possibility of one suspect for all the murders. For all we know at this point, there could be more than one murderer...with a common goal of killing the rich. We..."

Harris interjected. "Did you come up with a suspect profile that can shed some light in either direction?"

"Nothing of any use so far. I can give you the standard serial killer attributes in regards to gender, race, approximate age, etcetera...or that he or she lacks empathy and remorse, and is an impulsive narcissist. We've seen some of these traits in our cases, but not consistently. Many serial killers evolve as they perfect their routine, but this killer is different."

The captain sat forward with his face in his hands, propped by his elbows on the desk. "I can't speak for everyone but I'm not following you. Please enlighten me, Detective."

"Okay. I'll start from the beginning. Detective Scott brought the matter to my attention. It comes down to our homicide statistics and the fact there are a lot of wealthy people in the greater Detroit area—over a hundred thousand millionaires and a dozen or so billionaires."

Abigail's statement caught everyone except Ackley by surprise. She continued. "And we all know about our murder rate. The victims are usually from the middle and lower caste. Statistically, the wealthy aren't normally murder victims. As you can see from this list of ten names, all been killed in the last few months, it is quite an anomaly."

Knudsen put up his hand to ask a question, although it was more likely he was using the gesture to bring levity to the grim situation. He addressed Brown. "What are the numbers for...beside some of the victims?"

Scott turned to Campbell and whispered. "Did Simon talk about that?"

The Hun overheard him and asked, "Who's Simon?"

Brown glanced at Campbell and gave her half a head shake. "We have no idea what the numbers represent...they were left at the crime scenes, in various forms. They could be a clue, used by some serial killers to taunt police. We haven't had much luck with forensics either, some results are just coming in but nothing has produced any viable leads so far. As you can see, the cause of death in each and every case is different."

The captain threw himself back in his chair and folded his arms across his chest. "So, that's it. You want to tell the mayor we think a serial killer, or killers, are responsible for his friend's death because he was part of an exclusive club, murdered for no reason other than his financial status?"

Abigail raised her brow and shrugged. "No, sir. I'm only bringing you up to speed on our open investigations, and what we've learned so far. Telling the chief and mayor is your job."

Zawadski got up from his chair, gave the lieutenant a 'what the hell was that' stare, and stormed out of his office.

Bewildered, Harris watched him walk away. She turned to Brown, offering only a blank expression. "Thank you, Detective, that will be all for now. The rest of you can get back to work...I'll hand out specific assignments once I figure out how to handle this.

36
Fire

It wasn't surprising Norbert Lee's death didn't get more press coverage; just another un-noteworthy killing in murder city. Thick black smoke from the car fire attracted gawkers from the nearby freeway, and even the Channel 7 news chopper. It hovered over the raging inferno for fifteen minutes, I guess they didn't get enough gory footage to make the six o'clock news.

I'm proud of my quick work, doctoring the prick's vehicle with just the right cocktail of accelerants. It was thrilling to see how quickly the raging fire engulfed Lee and his SUV. I researched the best method to torch a vehicle, but only got to practice once on an abandoned junker.

The crowd that gathered around the burning car made it easy for me to watch. It was like the Keystone Cops, when the black pig chased the kid on the bicycle. For some reason, they suspected him of starting the fire.

Norbert Lee deserved to suffer, and he did. I watched him squirm, trying to escape the flames. They consumed him. I never saw anyone burn in a fire before. The melting flesh was surreal, like a wax figure in a horror movie.

A few brave souls tried to rescue him. They could only stand by and watch as he was cooked like a well-done steak. The fire extinguishers did little to quell the blaze, and the intense heat kept everyone at bay. An exploding airbag sent some scrambling for cover.

As usual, the fire department arrived just in time to cool down the hunk of glowing metal and molten plastic. When they got to Lee, what was left of him resembled a barbequed mannequin. They couldn't tell if the corpse was male or female. A salesman, who saw him before the fire, identified the man.

My fake license plate fell to the pavement when the rear bumper melted. I smirked when one of the detectives picked it up and bagged it as evidence.

It's become a challenge, trying to imagine, and planning how to kill each of my victims. Doing it from a distance has its advantages. The rush-job on Humboldt in the alley had me worried about blood spatter, getting so up close and personal. It was satisfying in the moment, but too risky. I want to continue my mission without being caught and I am aware how the cops hold back certain information, like DNA evidence, but I'm confident none was left behind. Vacuuming my clothes, shaving closely, and combing loose hair from my head, are all part of preparation. Interchangeable, cheap, and disposable clothes are also routine, along with latex gloves, and headgear or a hoody.

The goons in blue are stupid as far as I'm concerned. Forensic evidence solves most of their cases. I'm cognizant of that, and I know they'll never figure out the numerical clues I left behind. It's not that I'm trying to get caught. It is personal, and each number has a special meaning for each particular victim.

They are rich and shameless and must die for the suffering they have caused.

37
Freaky

Ackley followed Abigail back to her office and sat in the chair in front of her desk. "Okay, partner...I'm still your partner, aren't I...sort of? Who the heck is Simon and what do you and Lynda know about the numbers that I don't?"

Abigail sighed. She picked up a coffee cup from her desk she'd forgotten about and checked to see if it was still warm. "Shit, it's ice cold." She smiled at Ackley. "Yes, I still consider you my partner, even if your wings have been clipped. Simon is the psychic Lynda and I went to see last night."

"What?"

"I know...I know...I'm the last one to believe in that shit but this guy was different; scary different, and accurate."

Ackley stifled a laugh but couldn't resist a 'yeah, right' smirk. "Cards, tea leaves, or a crystal ball?"

"Would I shit you? The guy was five-foot fuck-all, Lebanese, the shy and quiet type. All he did was stare at the floor, and blow us away by relating images of people we knew, and what was happening in our lives. Simon didn't know who we were before meeting us, and only had Lynda's first name. He told us things no one could ever guess."

Ackley sat back and folded his arms across his chest. "You're serious. Like what?"

"My father, dead partner, uncle, last relationship..."

"Whoa, really? That's sick. What about numbers...you and Lynda were talking about it...the numbers left by our killer?"

Abigail still had the coffee cup in her hands. She popped the lid and checked inside, hoping it had miraculously reheated itself, and tossed it into the garbage pail. "I dunno...I think so. He said he saw random numbers, money, and a guy reading a newspaper. I'm still trying to put it all together in my head."

"You're kidding me?"

"I kid you not...it was freaky. He told Lynda stuff that blew her away too. If he guessed or made it all up, I would have asked for the winning lottery numbers. The guy really sees things."

"Did you ask any questions...about the numbers or our killer?"

"It doesn't work like that. He just sees shit and tells you about it...he even mimicked me typing and holding a gun."

Ackley wasn't sure what to say. He turned to the list of victims on the wall and stared at it.

"Freaky...like you say...but way cool. I guess it's hard for me to believe because I wasn't there, but I trust you. Honestly, I've always been open minded to things like that; phenomenon we can't explain. Who am I to say Simon's a fraud, if you and Lynda believe him? So, what's next?"

"Coffee and something to eat...let's hit the diner across the street. I need brain food to keep focused. This shit's getting heavy."

38
Catching

There was a note waiting on Abigail's desk when they got back from the diner. The lieutenant wanted to see her and Scott ASAP. She hung her purse on the back of her chair and hailed Ackley on the way to Harris' office. He had just sat down. Scott shrugged, got up, and followed her across the room.

Engrossed in her paperwork, the Hun had her head down. A funny picture ran through Abigail's mind. From that angle, with her thinning hair, protruding ears and rolls of neck fat, she resembled a Shar Pei. "You wanted to see us, LT?"

Harris didn't bother to raise her head and continued reading lines on a document with the assistance of a plastic ruler. "Yes, I've already told the others...everyone's to make a list of their top ten suspects for each of the wealthy victims. You too, Crunch...and work us up a viable suspect profile we can use for comparison. Hacker, see if there's anything to connect any of our victims."

"I already looked at that, LT, there's..."

"Look again...dig deeper. Take everyone's suspect lists and cross-reference those...something's gotta give." Taking pause from reading, she waved the ruler in the air as if she was conducting an orchestra. "And get on forensics...maybe they've come up with something we can use. Crunch, you created this mess...you're the OIC. The others have been told to coordinate with you."

The two detectives turned to leave the lieutenant's office, but Harris asked Brown to stay a minute and waited for Scott to disappear. "You mentioned someone named Simon, this morning. Who is he and what's that about?"

Abigail froze, unsure how to answer the question. "Umm...a friend in the FBI Behavioral Unit. I ran the different MO's and random numbers by him."

"And what does the Simon say?" Harris chuckled. "That's funny."

"He wasn't much help but offered to help with the profile. I told him to keep it between friends for now. I know how the department hates when the Feds get involved."

"So, nobody knows nothin about the numbers? Can't Hacker run some magic formula or alfarythym or something to figure it out?"

"You mean algorithm?"

The Hun waved Abigail off. "Don't sass me girl, you know what I mean...computers in my day were called slide rules."

"Don't you mean an abacus, LT?"

Harris furled her lower lip and feigned getting up from her chair.

Abigail giggled, and high-tailed it out of her office.

39
C

Days passed with no new millionaire murders, and little in the way of leads. Even the forensic experts were scratching their heads, feeling pressure to come up with anything they could call evidence. The majority of DNA samples collected belonged to victims. It was the same with fingerprints. There were some glove prints left by common latex gloves and a few partial prints found on Humboldt's quarters, but not enough for any kind of comparison.

The best forensic evidence so far, were the skin cells on Bulmer's rope. There was enough DNA for a profile but no matches came back from any available database. The entire major case squad was frustrated. Usually, they could rely on modern science and forensics to help solve their cases. Those were simple crimes committed by simple criminals. It seemed the homicide detectives were going to have to solve their cases the old-fashioned way, with solid police work.

Bruce Dunn stopped for a red light and turned to his partner. "Harry, you awake?"

Cummings grunted. He refused to wear sunglasses and always squinted so it was sometimes difficult to tell if his eyes were open or closed.

"This is bullshit...chasing down leads on our own case, but reporting back to Queen Abigail. Why is she in charge of our case, don't they think we can handle it on our own?

Shit, you probably have more time on lunch than she's got on the job, hey old man? I heard she got her own partner killed. They had a thing and he took a bullet for her."

Cummings held his gaze ahead, somewhere in the distance. "When you've been around here long enough, junior, you'll understand you can't believe everything you hear, and only half of what you see."

"What the hell is that supposed to mean? Is that some jarhead shit you picked up in the jungle?"

"If you have to ask, you haven't figured it out yet. Live and learn, kid. Brown knows what she's doing on and off the battlefield. She shielded a civilian in Afghanistan when an IED went off nearby. Luckily, her Kevlar saved both of them from shrapnel. Takes balls to do that for someone you don't even know. She also took down a serial killer not too long ago, when you were buying dime bags from gang bangers. The perp was an ex-cop with an impressive kill list."

"Huh. I'd heard she climbed the ladder because of her uncle...an ex-chief or something."

"There you go again...believing everything you hear. How many more names have we got on our queue for today?"

Dunn pulled to the curb and scanned their clipboard that listed persons of interest. "Computer boy made this up; like we couldn't come up with our own suspects. He's an anomaly for sure. How the hell did he ever make detective and what's he doing in major case?"

"He got shot, and knows more about computers than you do about shin splints."

"What the hell kind of comparison is that? He pointed to a name on their list. "Jeremy Hines. He's my number one pick. I don't care about the other dudes...I think this one is our torch. Wouldn't it be great to solve our own case? You know they call us the C Team?" That ain't for Cummings...we're in last place in the office race."

Harry glanced over at the clipboard in his partner's lap. "So, why is Hines our guy?"

"I did my own homework. Computer boy put him here because he was a disgruntled employee the vic downsized out the door. Just so happens my cousin worked at the same electronics store and gave me another connection to our dead guy. Seems Mr. Lee had a bit of a coke habit, and our man Hines was his connection. According to my cousin, Lee was tighter than a frog's ass, and he owed Hines money for dope. I guess he figured he'd dump the debt by doing the same to his dealer. How messed up is that? Then the stingy prick applied for a restraining order against Hines but got it wrong and the paper was issued for Jeremy Haines—last name spelled wrong. Our computer boy obviously missed this info."

Cummings nodded along in agreement. "Sounds like you've got something there, partner. Let's have at him. Where does he live?"

"On West Chicago."

Harry scrunched his face in thought. "Less than a mile from where Lee got barbequed.

The C Team parked out front of Hines' four-story apartment building.

Cummings groaned as soon as he walked in the front door. "Of course, it's on the top floor and there's no elevator...ain't that always the way."

Dunn took the stairs two at a time and didn't glance back until he hit the third floor. "C'mon Harry, you can make it." The Bulldog slowed his ascent, allowing his partner to close the gap. Dunn was almost at the apartment door when Cummings made it to the last flight up.

A young black male exited Hines's unit and brushed past Dunn on his way down the stairs. The former drug cop recognized the cocaine eyes, and caught a whiff of body odor that went along with a crack binge.

Bulldog knocked on the door just as his partner made it to the landing in front of Hines' apartment. The door flew open and a light-skinned African-American said, "You couldn't have smoked that already. The man appeared to be about thirty-five years of age and matched the description of Jeremy Hines. He was holding a wad of cash and a plastic baggie of little white rocks.

Dunn had seen his share of crack cocaine and drug deals during his time in narcotics. He reached through the open door to grab Hines. "Police, you're under..." The murder suspect ducked back into his apartment, dragging Dunn with him.

The door slammed shut before Cummings could get to it. He tried the handle to no avail. Hines and Dunn were struggling against the inside of the door. It suddenly flew open and knocked Harry backwards, down the top flight of stairs. He tumbled head over heal to the next landing.

Hines ran out the door and down the stairs with the former sprinter in pursuit. Seeing Cummings blocking the lower landing, Hines reached for a gun tucked in the front of his pants.

Harry tried to get his pistol, but he was laying on the holster and couldn't move his leg.

Dunn shouted, "Stop, Police!"

Cummings saw Hines pull the gun and turn toward his partner. He feared Dunn didn't see the weapon. The pain in his leg was extreme but instinct and training took over. The old detective was called a lot of things in his day; names like sleepy, piss tank, and old man. But, back in the day, he had been a crack shot in the military, and the Detroit Police pistol team champ for eight years running.

Cummings wrestled his weapon from its holster and took aim at center mass. Just as Hines raised his gun to shoot Dunn, the old warrior squeezed the trigger. It was weird, he thought, how he didn't hear the shot. His M16 had been so loud, whenever he let it loose in jungle in Viet Nam. The noise at the shooting range was deafening. The current silence had something to do with stress and tunnel vision.

Both of Hines' legs gave out and he fell face first, landing two steps below Bulldog, the revolver still clutched in his hand. The young detective stared at the weapon and kicked it out of the dealer's hand. Hines didn't move. Blood spilled from his upper abdomen and slowly made its way down the stairs toward Cummings. Dunn looked down at his partner and nodded.

Harry nodded back. "Call an ambulance, partner."

"For this piece of shit? He can bleed out right here."

"For me, Bruce...my leg's busted."

40
Heroes

The way Bruce Dunn was treated the next day, you'd think he'd just taken down Charles Manson. He spent the better part of the morning with Internal Affairs, being grilled about his involvement in the shooting. He showed up in major crimes looking as dapper and demure as an Armani model, donning the latest in men's fashion.

Lieutenant Harris was just leaving the office, heading to the vending machines for her first sweet fix of the day when her protégé came strutting in. Momentarily at a loss for words, she patted him on the shoulder. As he passed, she said to nobody in particular, "That's my boy." The Hun carried on while detectives in the room moved in for congratulations, offering more backslaps, handshakes, and praise for a job well done.

No one bothered to ask about Cummings, or how he was doing in the hospital. They had received a quick update from the captain first thing that morning, saying the veteran suffered multiple fractures to his leg, but he would recover.

Zawadski added he couldn't comment on the shooting because it was still under investigation, but he overemphasized a wink and told the troops it would all work out.

Abigail Brown sat on the corner of Ackley Scott's desk, watching the rookie detective accept accolades for what amounted to almost being killed and having his partner save his life. She scoffed at the irony. Brown heard from a friend at the hospital Cummings was in for a long rehab. Knowing how the department worked, she had no doubt he would be pensioned off for being too old and unfit for duty. It was when someone congratulated Dunn on catching the killer, her ears perked up.

Seeing the captain had joined the group, and realizing it was his words she'd just heard, Abigail almost fell off the desk. A search warrant at Hines' apartment resulted in evidence that could make him a viable suspect in the death of Norbert Lee. It might have been enough to charge him for it, if he wasn't dead. But there was no known connection to any of the other victims. She couldn't help herself and made her way to the gathering. "Did I miss something, Captain, do we have new evidence confirming Hines killed Lee, or that suggests he's tied to any of our other victims?"

Taken by surprise, Zawadski turned to Detective Brown. "Well, I know it may be a bit premature...but with the gun, the drugs, and the threatening emails recovered from his laptop, I'd say we will have this thing wrapped up in no time. It's not as if he was innocent...he tried to shoot a police officer. I've already told the mayor it's only a matter of time before we tie him to the Delancey case."

Abigail wanted to respond but thought it unwise. She felt a slight floor tremor and noticed the lieutenant shifted her weight. The stunned look on Harris' face said she was thinking the same thing. His statement was the stupidest thing she'd ever heard. Harris kept her mouth shut too and only shook her head in disbelief. Noticing Brown eyeballing her, she nodded toward her office.

The Hun had half of a date turnover in her mouth by the time Abigail got to the office. Harris caught falling crumbs with her free hand. "Please tell me my hunger pains affected my hearing and our Captain didn't just say he told the mayor we're about to wrap up the millionaire murders. Never mind, I know what I heard. What the hell is the matter with that man?" She looked past Brown to make sure her words didn't carry past the office door. "I hope I'm not around when he makes chief. He'll be the ruin of us all...he has never conducted an investigation of any kind. I swear...he couldn't find a killer in a room full of death row inmates."

Abigail wasn't sure how to respond or if she should, so she didn't. She took the empty seat in front of the lieutenant's desk and watched her guzzle a half can of coke to wash down her snack. A bit embarrassed by her superior's lack of couth, Brown stared at the dribble on her lower lip and the crumbs on her blouse.

The Hun wiped her mouth with the back of one hand and ignored any other spillage. She plopped her bosom on the desk and leaned forward. "What do you think about this Hines caper, detective?"

"Honestly, LT, I think they got Hines in the right place at the wrong time—in the middle of a drug deal. End of story. Would I consider him a *suspect* in Norbert Lee's death? Absolutely...any good detective would be a fool not to. If you're asking me if he's responsible for killing the other millionaires...my answer is no. He's not our man."

"Do you think he could've done Lee and it had nothing to do with the others?"

"Definitely not...doesn't fit the pattern..."

"What pattern? I thought you said there wasn't one?"

"I don't mean MO or cause of death. I know revenge plays a big part in this, but take Lee's license plate for example. Why put a fake tag on his car...with different numbers? This thing is all about the numbers, they are the key. Once we figure out what they mean or how they come into play it will point us to our real suspect."

"I hope you're right, Crunch, I'm counting on your expertise. I've put my share of bad guys away, but I have to admit this serial killer stuff is beyond my skill set. And if you ever tell anyone else that I said that, I'll deny it and transfer your ass to traffic enforcement. Now go find your partner and find me a killer. By the way, who's that weird looking kid I saw with Hacker?"

Abigail turned and looked across the office to Ackley's desk. "That's Julius...Jason...I forget his name, he's Ackley's little brother. I thought he cleared it with you; the 'bring your kid to work day' or something like that?"

"He did, but that is no kid."

"He's special needs, autistic I think...works at a book store. Ackley's his mentor I guess."

"Whatever, just make sure he stays out of the way...and don't let him eat the last Kit Kat bar in the vending machine, I've got my eye on it for my next snack."

Abigail was already on her way out the door. "Got it, LT...no Kit Kat."

41
Rain

Abigail spent the next hour looking for crime scene similarities in photos, comparing bodies for possible posing, wounds, and clothing styles. Clues come in all forms, and even though she felt the mystery numbers were the key, there had to be a reason for killing each of the victims. Were they murdered, simply because they were rich? The numbers; her head hurt from so much thinking. She needed brain food.

Seeing Ackley engaged with his special brother, Abigail walked over to Lynda Campbell's desk. "Hey, Lynn, I'm starving...wanna get some lunch?"

"I'd love to Abs, but Knudsen's on his way back from court, and we're hoping to pare down our suspect list. The captain worked everyone in the room, thinking he can force this investigation to an end."

Ackley overheard their conversation and spoke up. "I can do lunch."

Abigail turned. "Oh, I thought you were busy with..."

"Justin. He already ate...has his own schedule...remember?"

"Sure. Can you leave him here alone?"

"He'll be fine. We're working on cross-referencing names on the suspect lists and he's playing with an algorithm he whipped up. He's light years ahead of me when it comes to writing code."

Abigail let her eyes roam from Ackley to Justin, and then to Lynda. "Oh, yeah, I play with that in my spare time too." She and Lynda laughed. Justin's focus never left the computer screen. His fingers worked like he was competing in a speed-typing contest.

"You two go ahead." Lynda said. "I'll keep an eye on him."

Abigail and Ackley turned toward the door. Scott thought about telling Justin he was leaving, but the kid was so engrossed in his work he probably wouldn't notice his big brother's absence. Ackley lengthened his stride to keep pace with Abigail. He practically had to jog to stay close.

They went to the diner across the street. Abigail caught sight of the chalkboard near the door and called out to the woman behind the counter...she'd have the soup and sandwich special. She moved to a table and sat down. Ackley froze in front of the makeshift menu, trying to make a decision. Unsure of what he wanted; he grabbed a menu off the counter before joining his partner. He removed his suit jacket and settled in just as Abigail's soup arrived. "Jeez, that was quick. I don't even know what I want yet."

Abigail inhaled a spoonful of broccoli cheddar before answering. "I'm in here a lot and Debbie knows I'm either hungry or in a hurry." She nodded toward the owner/cook/waitress. "She runs the place and usually knows what I want before I ask for it...must be psychic."

Ackley scanned the menu as Debbie called out to him. "Rueben with kettle chips?"

He looked up at Abigail, wide-eyed, as if he'd just seen Elvis. "That's exactly what I was thinking...how could she know that?"

Debbie placed Abigail's triple grilled cheese sandwich in front of her. Brown wiped the corner of her mouth with a napkin. "Beats me."

Still slack-jawed, Ackley gawked at Debbie. "Okay, a Rueben sounds great, do you have…"

"Pumpernickel? Sure, no problem. Coming right up."

He watched her in awe, his eyes following her moves behind the counter, working in the tiny kitchen. "Amazing…and she's easy to look at too."

"Forget it. I know you haven't gotten laid in a while, but she's not your type."

"What do you mean, how would you know that?"

"Your sexual frustration shows, and you don't have a vagina."

Refueled, the A Team made their way back to the cop shop. Ackley was being his nerdy self, rambling on about Debbie and psychics and wondering to himself what else he knew nothing about. Abigail let it go in one ear and out the other. She was on her own channel, running photos, names, and comparisons through her brain.

When they walked back into the office, the Hun called out to them. The duo stopped at her doorway. "Two things, people: That better not be my Kit Kat bar he's eating…and what the hell is Rain Man doing in your office, Detective Brown?"

They turned to see Justin writing on the white boards where they'd listed victims, causes of death, and the mystery numbers. As if drawn by a powerful magnet, the A Team were pulled in that direction. Lynda Campbell was nowhere in sight and Justin was busy making notes alongside the victims' names and numbers. The detectives stood silent, watching him work, wondering what the young man was doing.

Ackley was embarrassed and worried his partner would be upset if his little brother messed things up. "Justin, what are you doing? That's important police work."

The kid was focused and on a mission. He didn't answer.

Ackley stepped closer to ask Justin again.

Abigail put a hand on his shoulder. "Wait...look at what he's done...his figures...check out the column on the right...beside our mystery numbers. If I'm not mistaken, those are dates."

42
Credit

Ooh, another white cop kills another black man. Is this what's considered news these days? I skimmed the story while working the New York Times crossword. Puzzles are one of life's challenges I still enjoy. On second thought, that isn't quite true. I also enjoy my new hobby, killing wealthy assholes.

It wasn't until I recognized the name of the electronics store where the victim, Jeremy Hines, worked, that I read the article. The dead man's name means nothing but his previous place of employment does. It's one of the companies Norbert Lee took over. Police say they interrupted a drug deal. Hines pulled a gun on one of their detectives and the cop used deadly force to defend himself.

The investigative reporter says the cops were investigating a murder, and Hines was a possible suspect. According to the reporter's source, the victim threatened his previous employer after his lay off. I sympathize with the man, completely understanding how he feels about the corporate raider who ruined his life.

The journalist left the article open-ended, as if there is more to come. I wonder if it is simply a cheap tactic to sell more papers, or if the reporter is any good at his job. The situation is something to monitor. Maybe an anonymous telephone call would push him in the right direction.

The keystone cops know by now someone is knocking off the wealthy. But they are remaining tight-lipped about it, probably afraid of an outcry from those with the clout to be heard. No doubt, the reporter would eat up such information...an interesting thought. I pulled my laptop closer and googled the name of the article's author.

Matt Jackson is a freelance journalist who writes his own blog and occasionally supplies police related stories to major newspapers. I scrolled through another piece he wrote on corruption in the Detroit mayor's office. It appears Jackson has a good source in the police department. There's no way that information came from the general public.

After skimming another political story about non-existent city services in Detroit, I wonder if the police source is also connected to the mayor's office, or vice versa. Either way, Jackson might be my man if I need to reach out for accolades in the millionaire murder investigation. I don't want anyone else taking credit. *The Millionaire Murders* would make a great headline.

I have time for one more math puzzle before signing in to the games room. The whiz kid, Jason, keeps outscoring me and it's time for revenge.

43
Second

"How long do we have to be the "B" Team? Brown's flying solo these days, with geek-boy grounded. Shouldn't we be the "A" Team now?" Knudsen was riding shotgun, fussing with something in his hands, while he looked out the passenger window.

Campbell tried to see what he was up to, but had to keep her eyes on the road. She didn't need him to comment on her driving, especially since she made a point of grabbing the car keys before he had a chance. She glanced in his direction, froze for a second, and nearly rear-ended the car in front of them. Her partner had something stuffed inside his lips to puff them out, his eyes were wide open and bulging, and he slouched in his seat to force his stomach out and look fat.

"Who am I?" He asked. Knudsen was a good cop, but a much better clown. His facial expressions alone could make Campbell laugh.

She corrected the distance to the car in front of her. "I hope that's not the LT's chocolate bar?"

He maneuvered the chocolate Kit Kat finger from behind his lip, to between his teeth, as if he was smoking a chocolate cigarette. "I found it."

"Where...in Harris' desk drawer?"

"I was hungry and I missed lunch...she doesn't need it."

"She'll castrate you if she finds out."

"The LT won't miss it...she's got a whole stash hidden in her bottom drawer. Did you know she goes to waist-watchers? I think she's *wasting* her money."

Campbell shook her head. There was never a dull moment, working with the Square Head. He was so deadpan. She never knew when he'd say or do something stupid to make her laugh. Lynda could've done worse for a partner. In fact, she'd worked with some real dicks. She enjoyed working with Karl. He treated her as an equal, and liked to have fun.

He swallowed the last of the chocolate. "Do you think we'll catch another break with this serial thing? We sure bombed out with the black widow and her boyfriend. Look at all the attention Dunn's getting, and he only got a drug dealer killed. Fool thinks Hines was the one who killed all the rich dudes. He needs to get his head out of his ass."

"He's not really that thick, is he? I thought he was just playing along to be the hero for a day."

"Right...and his partner saved his ass. I heard he hasn't even been up to see the old timer in the hospital. That's just wrong. Sometimes I think Dunn did some of the dope he seized while in narcotics and fried his brain. Dude might have done okay there, but this is the big leagues. Shit, I kissed a lotta ass to get this job, and he gets brought in by the Hun. I'll just blame the missing Kit Kat bar on him."

"Are you done whining? Who's next on our list?"

"Let me see...Elmer Fudd, 231 East Wisconsin."

"What? Get serious."

"I ain't shittin' you...guy's name is Elbert Fromm...close enough. Hacker's notes say he's got history with Delancey...indirectly. Worked as a pharmacy assistant in one of the stores the vic bought out. Says here his father was a pharmacist there before he croaked. Apparently, Fudd went a bit crazy when he was let go...started throwing pills all over the place and said he'd come back one night and blow the place up. The police were called and they had to physically remove him."

Campbell made a Michigan U turn and headed in the direction of Fromm's address. "Any criminal record?"

"Nope...not even a parking ticket. File says he was still attending drug school but had to drop out when he got canned. Hacker checked his financials and found he claimed bankruptcy after his old man died...couldn't pay off the medical bills."

"So much for working in a pharmacy and getting cheap drugs."

"It ain't just the drugs...you ever see what it costs to spend time in the hospital these days? I feel for him...poor bastard."

Campbell hit the freeway to save time crossing town. "Will you still feel that way if he's the killer?"

"Hmm...good question...let me think about it while we eat? How about White Castle...the candy bar ain't cuttin' it."

231 East Wisconsin was a single-family dwelling, one in a row of similar-looking homes built by the same contractor to house soldiers returning from World War II. Some had been kept up nicely, but the Fromm residence was not one of them. The aluminum siding was faded, dinged, and patched to cover over old windows. Foreclosure and eviction notices were posted on the front door. The Detroit Police Detectives paused to read it before Knudsen knocked.

Campbell commented, "Guess that confirms things aren't going well for Mr. Fromm."

There was no answer at the door. All the curtains were drawn but Lynda saw movement when her partner knocked again. "Someone's in there, they know we're here."

Knudsen used his official police knock on the aluminum door, rattling the whole front of the house. It was enough to cause a neighbor to poke their head out in an attempt to see what was going on. Campbell flashed her badge. "Police...do you know if Mr. Fromm is around?"

The old woman dropped her chin to her chest and stepped back into her house. Knudsen switched from his knuckles to his fist and continued pounding on the door. A face appeared between the curtains. Campbell held her badge against the glass and the person disappeared. Finally, the inside door swung open and a man stepped up to the storm door.

"What do you want? I have another week to vacate."

Knudsen took the lead. "Can we come in and talk to you sir, it's not about your eviction." Fromm stood fast with his left hand on the door handle. Their information said he was thirty-three but he looked ten years older with premature grey hair, and deep creases lining his forehead. He wore a MSU tee shirt and faded jeans with holes in the knees.

"Can I see some ID from the both of you? Can't be too careful these days...especially with those sneaky repo bastards. They'll lie and say anything to get in...even took my father's TV because he died...he didn't make the last payment. Fucking scavengers...like buzzards to fresh road kill." Satisfied with their police credentials, Fromm let them into the house.

The detectives followed the person of interest into his living room, where he collapsed into a well-worn recliner. Packed boxes covered the sofa, matching chair and most of the floor space in the small room, leaving nowhere to sit. The detectives remained standing and Campbell surveyed the living area while her partner interviewed the man.

Fromm listened to Knudsen's questions but his eyes followed his partner's movements as she slowly edged further into his personal space. Ignoring the first two questions, he cut the male detective off. "As you can see, I'm kind of busy packing up the house, before they come and drag me out." He sighed and took in the clutter surrounding him. "Maybe you can tell me what exactly it is you want so we can all get on with our day."

Knudsen skipped the pleasantries and dropped the bomb. "Your old boss Lance Delancey was murdered recently and we're wondering what you might know about that?"

Campbell stopped in her tracks; a bit shocked by her partner's direct approach. She had been busy scoping out the room, trying to see what kind of person Fromm was. She checked him for his reaction.

He took a moment, as if thinking about what he was about to say. His eyes dropped to his lap, where he cupped his hands and picked at a hangnail on his thumb. "First of all, officer, that man wasn't my boss. My father worked for him years ago, when he only had one pharmacy, before he got rich and greedy and discarded all the people who helped him get that way. They were friends once, but when my father was dying in the hospital, the arrogant asshole couldn't find the time to visit him. "

Knudsen opened the wound and made no attempt to stop the bleeding. "So, you didn't like the man much?"

Fromm lifted his head but turned to Campbell when he answered. "He told my father he'd match contributions to my college fund, when I decided to follow in his footsteps.

It was another empty promise and all the money my dad had went to his medical bills. I even tried to get wholesale prices for some of his meds but that big shot wouldn't return my calls. He had his flunky, the store manager, handle the rejections."

With his subject agitated, Knudsen kept up the pressure. "We were told you went crazy and threatened to blow up the place when they let you go."

Fromm tensed up, wrung his hands, and leaned forward. "Let me go? They fired me because I dropped out of school...which had been part of the agreement to keep working there. I had to quit because I couldn't pay tuition. If I kept my job at the store, I might have been able to pull it off, but when my father died..." His voice got shaky and he stopped talking. Fromm covered his face with his hands. "Are we done? I really need to finish packing."

The detectives eyed each other. They were really only getting started. Since there weren't any grounds for an arrest, they would have to move on.

Knudsen spoke up. "One last thing, sir...where were you the night Delancey was killed?" The detective had a brain fart and looked to Campbell for the exact date.

She no sooner opened her mouth, and Fromm cut her off. "Really doesn't matter what night it was...I don't go anywhere and have been here, alone, packing...when I'm not sleeping. So, no...I didn't kill the rich bastard. Now, can you please leave?"

The detectives shared one last glance before turning to exit. Maybe the conversation could have gone better in the confines of a police interview room, but other than the verbal threat he made to the store he worked at, they had nothing else to use against him.

44
Code

Abigail quietly walked around her desk and sat down in her chair. Ackley stepped backwards, tripped, and practically fell into the empty seat in front of her desk. It was like watching Einstein working on his theory of relativity.

"Dates for what?" Scott inquired, "That's not when the killings occurred."

Brown gawked at the board and rubbed her chin, in thought. "I don't know...how do we ask him?"

"He doesn't like to be interrupted. We'll have to wait until he's done. Even when we work on puzzles, he has to do it his way in his own time. It's the same with everything he does whether he's eating, getting dressed, or working. Justin concentrates on one task at a time and completes it before he moves on to the next. It's the system he lives by and how he manages to function in society." Ackley wondered if Abigail was listening to anything he said.

She was as engrossed in Justin's work as he was. Her face twisted and narrowed.

"Look there." She pointed at two new numbers on the board, beside the names of Jerome Baylor and Brian Coulter, 1,409 and 1,980 respectively. "He's come up with two more...where the hell did those come from?"

Scott shook his head. He stared at his little brother in awe. It wasn't unusual for the young man to invoke that kind of reaction from him. Thinking he was of above average intelligence, Ackley often wondered about Justin's IQ. He couldn't be tested to obtain a number for comparison. His brain and its computing power remained a mystery.

As his mentor, Ackley found it difficult to challenge Justin. Normal word search and crossword puzzles were much too easy for him. He didn't like the game of chess, maybe because Scott was too slow at taking his turn. The kid's mind had to be engaged, even when he wasn't working on a problem or puzzle. His brain was in constant search mode.

Even after taking classes and receiving instructions on how to deal with Justin and his autism, Scott constantly worked at earning his trust and keeping his attention. He could tell when his words got through to the young man, but he was never quite sure how much he understood. Justin was on his own channel and Scott had to tune in to his frequency to communicate.

Brown turned to her partner. "Go grab your lap top and add Justin's figures to our list. Search the internet for those dates and see what pops. Do you think he can enlighten us when he's finished whatever it is he's doing?"

Scott shrugged, got up, and headed out to his desk. Abigail started at the top of the amended list and plugged in the first date into her computer. Her plan was to run it through the department's database and look for events or occurrences corresponding to the dates. She checked the white board, and continued entering the other dates. The computer did its thing. She watched Justin.

He created another column, squeezing it in beside the dates... he wrote more names. She waved to get Scott's attention, but he had his head down engrossed in his work.

Abigail dialed his extension and he looked up, recognizing her number.

45
Vibes

They stepped off the porch, heading to their car, when Campbell glanced back over her shoulder and saw Fromm close the front door. She wasn't sure, but thought he smirked when he turned his head. She turned to Knudsen. "Did you see that?" Two strides ahead of her and aimed at the street, it was obvious he didn't.

The joker didn't answer until they were in the unmarked. "See what?"

Campbell put the key in the ignition but didn't start the car. "Probably seeing what I wanted to...I think the bastard smirked at us when he shut the door. He was wound like an alarm clock...it looked like he was trying to pull his own fingernails out. He's definitely hiding something."

Knudsen chuckled. "And that surprises you? Everyone lies to the police. Don't you know, partner, a good investigator has to sort through the lies to find the truth. Nobody ever offers it for free...lie, deny, and lawyer. It's the American way."

She started the car and pulled from the curb. "I agree with all that...it's just the vibe I got from Fromm. Not just his anger over the shitty hand he's been dealt. It was what he didn't say...does that make any sense?"

"I caught the body language too, and agree he was holding back, but he didn't seem the revengeful type to me. Like the big kerfuffle he put on when they canned him at the pharmacy...all show and no go. He threw some pills around when he could have choked out the manager. Even if he blames Delancey, killing him is a big leap. Hey, we're close to the hospital...you wanna pop in and see Cummings?"

Campbell nodded and made the next turn to get them there. "I hear you. But my gut's telling me there's more to Elmer Fudd than meets the eye."

"Ha, listen to you...silly wabbit."

When the detectives asked the desk nurse for directions to Cummings' room, she said it was nice of them to come, since there had been very few visitors. He was sleeping when they got to the door. "There's a surprise," quipped Knudsen. His partner elbowed him in the ribs and brushed past. It was a double room but the bed beside the injured cop was empty. There were two get-well cards and a small plant on the nightstand.

Campbell dragged a chair closer to his bed, allowing its legs to scrape the floor and make noise. Cummings stirred and opened his eyes, blinking a few times to focus. He was groggy. "Hey, Lynda, it's nice of you to stop by...I just nodded off. Ya can't get much sleep around here with them coming in and out of the room every couple of hours to see if you're still alive."

He tilted his head toward the next bed. "That guy didn't make it through the night...poor bastard. How's your partner doing?"

Knudsen was standing on the other side of the bed, reading one of the cards. "I'm good, Harry, you enjoying the sponge baths...any hot nurses washing your balls?"

Cummings laughed and choked on his own saliva. He reached for his cup of water and took a sip. "I wish...the one washing me could be the Hun's twin." They all laughed. Campbell asked if the food was any good and he shrugged. "Not bad, I guess...about par with the TV dinners I eat at home. No booze though. I found it hard at first but this could be a good way for me to dry out."

The detectives made eyes at each other but didn't respond.

Cummings cleared his throat and continued. "Department sent a paper pusher in here to pension me off...said I'd never be cleared for active duty and they didn't have any more room for walking wounded. Asshole had the forms with him, and expected me to sign right then."

Campbell put a hand on his shoulder.

Knudsen replied. "That's your thanks for nearly getting killed on the job. Fuckers! What are you gonna do...any other options?"

"Maybe work security...like all the others that are too old and feeble. Actually, when Dunn and I were at one of the pharmacies talking to a POI, the manager waved me over and asked if I knew anyone in the security business to work his store. I'm thinking, maybe, I could do something like that...once I'm back on me feet. Any luck with finding our millionaire killer?"

Campbell shook her head.

Her partner answered. "Your idiot partner thought it was the guy you shot and he tried to take credit for solving the case. The captain actually bought it...if you can believe that."

"Dunn...that kid has a lot to learn. If he hadn't been in such a hurry, I wouldn't have had to kill Hines. Not that I'm all broken up about it, but he didn't deserve to die for slinging dope."

"C'mon, Harry." Knudsen offered. "He knocked you down the stairs and drew on you and your partner. You saved Dunn's life...I don't think he gets that."

"Oh, he does. Took him a few days but he finally came around and thanked me. He's got an ego the size of Belle Isle, and likes to show off with his fancy suits and all...but the kid means well. He knows he fucked up...won't admit it, of course." He scoffed. "Don't expect him to. I chalk it up to a lesson learned the hard way. I've made my share of mistakes."

Campbell stood up and glanced toward the door to signal her partner it was time to leave. "We've all made mistakes, Harry. I'm just glad it was the other guy who took a bullet, and you lived to tell the tale...another war story to share with the guys." She rounded the bed. "You get well and take it easy on the nurses. We gotta get back to work."

"Thanks guys...nice of you to come. Now go catch a killer."

Knudsen offered a mock salute.

Campbell waved goodbye and bumped into a big black nurse on her way out the door.

"It's time for your bath, Harold."

Lynda glanced back and wasn't quite sure, but it looked like Cummings was smiling.

46
Lunch

Ackley Scott got to his partner's office just in time to see his little brother finish whatever it was he was doing. Justin spun around; his eyes focused somewhere between the two detectives. "All done." With that short statement, he made another quarter turn and headed out the door. "Lunch time."

Justin carried the nonchalant expression directly to Ackley's desk, where he sat down, and opened his lunch bag. Justin removed a juice box and placed it in the two o'clock position in front of him. An apple came out next and went at eleven o'clock. Then he placed a sandwich directly in front of him and methodically unfolded the paper wrapping. Brown and Scott watched him, bewildered.

The detectives' fixation on Justin waned and they turned to each other, brows raised, wondering. Like identical twins, but of different gender, color, and parents, they turned to the board. Neither spoke. They completed another synchronized glance at Justin, and turned back to the list.

Abigail broke the silence. "What the hell does that kid know that we don't?"

Ackley didn't answer directly. He scanned the dates, new numbers and names. "Did you get anything from our police files?"

"No. You?"

"Nothing. The new numbers are a mystery, like the rest, but..."

"Can't you just ask him about what he wrote?"

"I dunno...maybe after his lunch. He doesn't do well with direct questions...or general conversation. He makes calculated statements. It's like talking to a computer sometimes." Ackley glanced in Justin's direction for a second. "I guess I can try...maybe I should call his mother and ask her advice...but she might freak if she hears he's helping us with a murder investigation."

Abigail nodded. "Yeah, you might want to leave that part out. We have to be careful not to leak anything about a serial killer to the public. What about the dates or new names?"

"That's what I was going to mention...the dates are still a question mark, but have another look at those names...they're companies, I think. 'Delta' is the name of Delancey's pharmaceutical company, if I'm not mistaken."

"You're not partner. 'Worldwide' is Bulmer's mega media corporation and I think 'Atlas' might be the name of Humboldt's muffler and lube shop empire. Shit! The Rain Man really is a genius."

"Hey...that's not..."

"I know, I'm sorry. I guess it stuck in my brain after the Hun said it." Her phone buzzed and she checked the message. "Forensics sent me a text...I'm gonna touch base with them before I bring the LT up to speed. Can you see if you can match up the other names with our victims and their kingdoms?"

"You got it, partner. I'll poke at Justin a bit and see if he can shed any additional light on his additions to our list.

What a kid. And if he can't, I'll try going around him to his mother...don't worry, I'll be discreet."

Abigail dialed up Forensics from her desk and her buddy Doug Cowper answered on the first ring. "Sitting on the phone, Skel? Shouldn't you be examining particulates through a microscope or something?"

"I'm multitasking. Saw your extension. Knowing how impatient you are, I grabbed the phone pronto. Didn't want to get into it with the text I sent you. I haven't finished my report yet but I got some good latents from the Coulter scene."

"Who?"

"Brian Coulter...the strangulation in Royal Oak?"

"Oh, yeah, shit. Sorry. I haven't quite caught up with that one. They shipped it over from the precinct after we identified it as another of the millionaire murderers. I'm swamped...we have ten on our list now."

She could hear Cowper flipping through paperwork on his desk. "Well, maybe I can help you a bit on this one...got two identifiable fingerprints from the Coulter crime scene and I found a match in the state database. Turns out the guy used to be a State Trooper...name of Connors, Michael."

47
Mike

Lynda Campbell and Karl Knudsen managed to knock off the five top names on their list. Some had alibis and some didn't. All had reason to speak out and hate their former employer. None seemed to be serious contenders for the title of millionaire murderer. Then again, the investigators didn't expect any of them to jump up and admit to it.

Late in the afternoon, the B Team headed back to the barn to write up reports on their individual interviews. Campbell wheeled through a drive through on the way in, grabbing a tray of coffees for their co-workers in the office. She turned to Knudsen, hoping he'd buy for a change, but he only gawked out his window.

In the major crimes' office, the gang was busy completing paperwork. Lynda dropped her purse and valise at her desk, and delivered the coffees.

Abigail watched her friend move around the room. Campbell caught Abigail's gaze and popped into her office. Brown accepted the coffee with a nod and waited for Lynda to sit down.

"This looks serious...what's up, Abs?"

"Mike Connors."

"What about him...did the black widow knock him off too?"

"We've got his prints at another murder scene."

"You're kidding me. Which one?"

"Coulter."

"Who?"

"That's what I asked. He was added to the list later...a strangulation in Royal Oak. I was just going over the file before you came in."

"Holy crap. His alibi for Delancey was solid and we had nothing else..."

"I know, I know, Lynn. Do you remember any mention of Brian Coulter...his limo or tour bus company?"

Campbell ran the name through her memory bank. "No, but I'll look back through my notes and ask my partner. Sounds like a really big coincidence and I know how you feel about those."

"There was no murder weapon but Connors' prints were found in the victim's home. Now that I've talked to you, I'm going to meet Sergeant Cowper in Forensics and we're going to have another look at the evidence and coroner's report."

"Do you want Karl and I to drag him back in here?"

"Not yet. Let's see what else shakes out...we need to get our act together, so he won't be as prepared this time. Nothing personal, but his last interview was a shit show. He was in control and he knew it, as if he was on our side of the table...must have been a good cop at one time. You still have any contacts with the State Police? What about that captain who was all over you?"

Lynda scoffed. "That asshole...heard he's counting fish somewhere up north, after screwing up on the Jensen case. I think one of the other investigators who worked with us is still in homicide. I'll make a call." She turned to leave and caught a glimpse of new writing on the whiteboard. "You've made some progress with the mystery numbers?"

Abigail nodded toward Ackley Scott's desk. "Justin added two numbers but we still don't know what the hell they are. We believe the names on the right are companies and corporations owned by the victims."

"What? How would he know that?"

"He's autistic... according to Ackley he has a knack for numbers and puzzles."

Campbell shook her head. "Do you think he's who Simon was talking about?"

Abigail only shrugged.

Lynda stared at the updated list on the whiteboard, as if she was contemplating something.

"Something bothering you, Lynn?"

"Just thinking about one of our interviews today...the guy worked for Delancey at one time."

"And he looks good for it?"

Campbell pinched the bridge of her nose, as if trying to subdue headache pain. "I dunno...something off about him. Never mind, I'll go and get into Connors again."

48
Spider

Doug Cowper loved his job in Forensics, but he'd never tell any of the upper echelon. He wasn't keen about being a supervisor in the unit; too much responsibly for things like budgets, keeping up with the latest technology, and quirky subordinates. At least one of them reported his grumbling and groaning to the big wigs. Maybe that was a good thing. If they knew Doug was happy, they would transfer him.

There was a time when if someone proved to be good at their job, or developed an expertise in a certain area, administration kept them in that position. But all good things come to an end. The powers to be decided no one should stay in any particular job more than five years for fear of 'pigeonholing'. Because of that decision expertise went out the window and the whole service was always in a state of flux, with new employees training constantly.

Cowper spent a number of years working the front lines, in uniform, but always wanted to try his hand at CSI. Once there, he excelled and gained expertise in various types of photography and videography, and specialized in blood spatter. He thought the fun was over when they promoted him to sergeant. It normally meant a return to the uniform division, but as luck would have it, department downsizing worked in his favor. They took away the lieutenant position, giving those duties and responsibilities to the sergeant, newly promoted Cowper. Taking the job meant accepting more responsibility, but it was his ticket to stay in the unit another five years.

The forensic specialist worked his fair share of murder investigations with Detective Abigail Brown, including a couple involving serial killers. Cowper considered her the best criminal investigator in the Detroit Police, and as far as he was concerned, she could easily fit in an organization like the FBI. He enjoyed working with Brown and considered her a friend.

The sergeant was concerned about her latest onslaught of cases, which everyone was calling the 'Millionaire Murders'. Normally organized, almost to the point of being obsessive compulsive, Brown appeared frazzled; overwhelmed with the collection of high-profile homicide investigations in her work queue.

The cases were not typical. Murder victims were usually from the lower caste and rarely missed by anyone. This time, all the victims were wealthy and connected. They had important friends, including members of government. Campaign contributions from certain victims supported these politicians. They offered their unwanted opinions, and put pressure on the police to get justice for their wealthy friends who perished so violently.

"Skel, where the hell are you?" Abigail Brown called across the cavernous room. There was no answer. She made her way across the office, poking her head into various cubicles and labs. She stopped beside a closed door when she heard someone on the other side of it cough. Letting herself into the room, the detective saw Cowper hunched over a microscope and wearing headphones. She crept up behind him and gently blew on the back of his neck.

The sergeant reached back with one hand and ran his fingers over the same spot.

Abigail tried not to laugh and did it again.

Cowper glanced up at a ceiling vent, appearing aggravated at the air blowing on him. He rubbed the spot on his neck again and adjusted his collar.

Brown was beside herself. She used the tip of a fingernail and slid it under his collar.

Cowper swatted the back of his neck and jumped up from his chair. He yanked the headphones off, spun around as if searching for an insect, and found Abigail standing there, hand clamped over her mouth to stifle her laugh. "You...you sneaky..."

"It's okay to swear and call me names, Skel."

"You scared the crap out of me. I thought for sure something was crawling down my shirt. We get some nasty-looking centipedes down here."

She laughed so hard her shoulders bounced up and down. "You crack me up...serves you right for wearing headphones. How are you supposed to hear visitors...or the phone?"

Cowper stood with his hands on his hips, shaking his head. "Are you just about done? That's' the whole idea and why the door is closed...I can't get any work done with interruptions or the phone ringing all day. Since the bean counters upstairs decided I didn't need a secretary, I've had to take on that job too...so much for my promotion."

Abigail picked up the discarded headphones and listened to one speaker. "Country and Western...really?"

"What's wrong with that? It relaxes me so I can concentrate on my work."

"Speaking of work...what've you got for me?"

Cowper walked over to the door and held out his arm. "Follow me, detective." He led her to a project room across the hall and motioned her inside. "Come see what I've done...just for you." He pointed at the far wall covered with whiteboard.

Abigail took a few steps toward it, stopped, and scanned the list the specialist had put together. "Wow...you've been busy." She read over the victim's names, with evidence collected at each crime scene. The investigator blew air from puffed cheeks. "There's not a hell of a lot there...nothing that links to one suspect?"

"That's not necessarily true. Thus, the reason I requested the list Ackley Scott put together...and then I expanded it. I know this case is huge and complicated, even for you, so I've put everything in your language to help you out. Now take a step back and look at my board again. You're the profiler, what do you see?"

"Bits and pieces of evidence that don't mean..." She stopped talking for a minute and focused on the wall as a whole. "Holy shit...I see it...Skel...you're a genius; pieces of a human puzzle. Foot print at Pearson scene, DNA from Bulmer's, smudged fingerprint from Humboldt, hand size from Coulter. You've built me an evidentiary profile...very cool, my friend."

Cowper nodded. "Yep, and I have a copy for you. I didn't want to send it up and ruin the surprise."

Abigail followed the technician's evidence and notes to the column on the far right. His findings and subsequent conclusions, spelled out a basic description of the killer; male, Caucasian, approximately 5'-10" in height, average build, right-handed with a 6-inch span from thumb to baby finger, writes numbers in script, has type O blood, and wears a size 9 shoe. "Shit, Skel, do you have an address for him?"

He smiled. "That would be geographic profiling. Your area of expertise, I believe. But I think it's safe to say he's from Michigan...probably the Detroit area."

Abigail threw her arms around Cowper and hugged him. He wasn't sure how to respond. "Can you send me a copy of this...I'll have to bring the LT and captain up to speed and update the troops."

He bent over the desk and hit the enter button on his laptop. "Done. I just sent it to your email. Oh...you remember how there were no identifiable prints on that roll of quarters...did you know they were all minted in 1976...another number for your collection?"

Abigail was already half-way out the door. "You're the best, Skel, catch you later..."

49
Moving

'Millionaire Murders in Motor City' The front-page story in the Free Press chastised the blue bozos for keeping the brutal killings quiet; not warning the public a serial killer was on the loose. The headline has a nice ring to it. Making a name for myself is something I hadn't considered since it was purely a personal thing.

If the media wants to give me a name, I won't lose any sleep over it. I'm not seeking notoriety and I never planned on getting caught, so why should I care if they give me a moniker for knocking off some of the rich and shameless. According to the paper, the mayor's office forced the cops to release the names of the victims. That slimy reporter gave out funeral arrangements on the latest one.

That sounds like fun; getting a close look at those in mourning and seeing how they feel after they lose everything. I have the details of the funeral service written down; and I'll attend. With the note in my pocket, I surveyed the near empty apartment. A day past the eviction date, I'm surprised no one has shown up to throw me out; typical Detroit bureaucracy.

The barren condition of my home is amusing. I stripped and either sold or tossed anything not bolted down—appliances, light fixtures, receptacle and switch plate covers, curtains and rods, the A/C unit, vent covers, and even the carpeting. I'll leave behind all the newspapers and food scraps from the previous two weeks. Ants are already marching in and claiming the kitchen as their own. I hope rats follow.

On my way out the door, I inserted the key into the deadbolt and broke it off. A final fuck you to the landlord, or the bank, or who ever took over the mortgage. Not quite satisfied, I gobbed on the door handle. Feeling a bit better, I tossed my backpack over a shoulder and headed to the street. My car was confiscated long ago, but I like walking. It gives me time to think.

The new place is a fair jaunt, but I can use the exercise. The abandoned building housed a pharmacy at one time, another victim of corporate greed. I worked a few shifts there to fill in for the assistant pharmacist, when she was away on vacation. They gave me a key for the back door that I conveniently forgot to return. The locks were never changed when the business closed for good.

The buildings on both sides are also vacant; owned by the same company that no longer exists. Other neighborhood businesses folded during the recession so the street is quiet and chances are no one will see me coming in or going out of the alley. No furniture and no hydro were left behind. Oddly though, the water has never been turned off; more typical behavior from a lax Detroit utility.

I attended Norbert Lee's funeral, mostly out of curiosity, wondering how they'd present someone who burned to a crisp. From what I saw the day of the fire, they should have let him burn a little longer, and simply scooped his ashes into an urn. It would have saved a lot of fuss and money.

The obituary said it would be a private family service, with internment at a family plot in Flat Rock. It took the taxi almost an hour to get me there. Cost wasn't a problem since I used Delancey's money to pay the fare. Disappointed for not considering it earlier on, but taking money from the rich and giving it to the poor made perfect sense. Being dead, my victim would never miss the money, and his widow probably wasn't aware of the hidden stash.

I watched the funeral service from a distance, from behind another rich bastard's tomb; I remembered how easily the pharmacy tycoon gave up the cash in consideration for his life. I chuckled to myself. *Sorry, I lied, and you died anyway.* Delancey probably hid the money from the taxman as well as his wife. Tempted to blow the stacks of hundred-dollar bills on frivolous things and a nice place to stay, I gave a chunk to the soup kitchen for those worse off than me, and I'll use the rest to finance my mission.

Using binoculars to get a closer look at the faces of the grieving family, I wasn't surprised to catch the widow with dry eyes. She was probably daydreaming about her inheritance. One reporter suggested the couple was on the outs and that Mrs. Delancey spent most of her time in Florida. Who really cares?

It was the old woman's grief; it caught in my throat, and eventually consumed me. Ready to collapse, young men on both sides held her up. Her face was soaked with tears and I could hear the sobbing. It brought back painful memories of my father.

I wished I could have done more to ease his suffering.

How could I cause another human being that much pain? What have I done to this poor woman? I didn't consider the collateral damage, and sense of loss. I should have known better, but the urge for revenge blinded me. Was the satisfaction of completing my mission worth the anguish

I caused others? A burning sensation in my chest said it was not.

50
Suspected

Abigail managed to catch the lieutenant as she was leaving for home. The Hun was in a hurry and didn't react to the news of a suspect description. She assured the detective she'd assemble the troops in the morning for a full briefing. Abigail shared her news with Ackley. He never went home until his partner did. He was happy to hear of some progress.

Justin couldn't offer any more insight. Ackley found not being able to communicate openly with his little brother frustrating. He knew it was the nature of Justin's illness.

Ackley had Abigail forward him a copy of Cowper's list. He would have a closer look at it when he got home.

With nothing pressing to do, they walked out together.

Still feeling high in the morning, from the previous day's visit with Cowper, Abigail arrived at the office feeling taller. Taking in the room, she was surprised at how large the task force had grown. Being focused and so busy, she never noticed how many detectives had been assigned to the millionaire murders; borrowed or seconded from other investigative units across the city.

Brown was settling at her desk, when Lieutenant Harris walked into her office and wedged herself into the chair. She wore a pink pantsuit and blouse. One of her fat rolls squeezed out between the vest and slacks, like a cracked tube of Pop 'n Fresh Dough. "Everybody but the captain is here. The boss wants me to call him when we're about to start...he's upstairs, probably kissing ass before the next round of promotions. He feigned interest in your new suspect profile."

"I didn't think you were listening, when I filled you in last night."

"I heard you, Crunch, and I was listening. That's the same persona I use when my husband talks to me...sorry. You ready to address the troops?"

"Yes, ma'am."

The Hun hated that word and shot Brown a dirty look on the way out the door. Harris hollered across the room, as if she was trying to round up cattle. It worked. Everyone stopped what they were doing and directed their attention to the front of the room. Abigail took her queue and asked them to refer to the whiteboard Ackley prepared prior to the briefing.

A new column had been added, written in red letters. A basic description of their suspect, compiled by bits and pieces of evidence collected from the different crime scenes. Muffled conversation resonated throughout the room as various investigators digested the new information. Someone asked if the DNA could provide more personal details, such as race or family heritage. It was a good question, considering new advances in testing and technology.

"Our local testing facility is limited." Brown replied. "But I'll see if the FBI lab can do better."

Captain Zawadski walked into the room and curled his upper lip; obviously not happy the meeting started without him. He spoke up. "What about Mike Connors, Detective, does he fit that profile?"

Brown refrained from telling her boss what she really thought about his half-baked theory. She turned to Campbell. "Lynn...what do you think?"

"Pretty close...but he's taller and he's..."

The captain cut her off. "We have his prints at another crime scene...why aren't you bringing him back in? Maybe in handcuffs he'd sing a different tune this time."

Knudsen chimed in. "Would if we could, Cap, he's MIA. Seems Delancey's widow was anticipating a divorce and parked all her money in a Cayman Islands account in Connors's name so hubby didn't have access to it. According to my source in Miami, Connors cleaned out the account and fell off the grid. Rumor is, he bought a boat and sailed off to parts unknown."

The captain threw his hands in the air. "With his prints at two murder scenes, he seems the likely suspect to me."

Campbell picked up. "We have an explanation for that, sir. According to the other victim's wife, Jenny Coulter, Mike Connors worked part-time security for him before Delancey."

"Weren't the prints recovered in the bedroom? Sounds like the man got around."

"Yes, he did, sir. The widow eventually admitted she and Connors had a fling while he worked for her husband. Brian Coulter became suspicious and told the ex-cop his services were no longer required."

Zawadski eyeballed Lieutenant Harris. "Isn't that just dandy...our best suspect was banging two of the victims' wives and now he's disappeared with a shitload of the mayor's best friend's money. I can't wait to tell him." He shook his head in disgust, turned, and stomped back to his office like a pouting child just cut from the soccer team.

Silence hung in the air for another moment, while everyone watched the captain leave.

Abigail continued. "Take another look at your suspect lists, people...see if any of them match our profile. I know it probably describes half of them, but it's another piece of the puzzle...putting a face to this killer. Does anyone have someone who comes to mind...someone you may have already interviewed?"

Lynda Campbell didn't respond, but thought about the guy who was being evicted. That cartoon character, what was his name? Elmer Fudd. How could she forget that? Brown took questions from two other investigators, so Lynda kept her thoughts to herself. She made a mental note to discuss her suspicions with her partner and maybe, take another crack at him. Campbell knew they had to exhaust all avenues to find Conners too.

51
Grieving

Erin O'Reilly spent her days working on her tan, and most of her nights at the Parrot Cay Yacht Club in the Turks and Caicos. Today was different. She lounged in a white wicker basket chair on the private dock, sipping a Gin Rickey, staring across the azure waters of the Caribbean Sea. When the friendly neighborhood dolphins didn't distract her, Erin gazed through her binoculars, awaiting her special guest.

A young black man, dressed in white cotton pants and a matching form-fitting golf shirt, appeared briefly to see if she needed a drink refill or if lunch would be for one or two people. He had been told to expect a guest sometime that day, but there was no need to ready the spare bedroom. She would be entertaining in her personal suite.

Not really sure how she was supposed to feel during the grieving process, Erin picked up her cocktail glass and marveled at how the sun shone through the ice cubes, making little rainbows in each one. The sky beyond her glass appeared blurry; maybe it was the alcohol affecting her vision. She didn't care. He would be there soon.

The police said her father was killed in a hit and run accident. They later changed their story, saying it may not have been an accident after all. If Kelly O'Reilly was murdered, it didn't make any difference in how she felt about the man. Legally he was her father but there was never any emotional connection. Erin didn't believe her father emotionally connected with anyone, including her mother.

Her parents told her they remained married for financial reasons and they lived separate lives. Mom checked in on Erin from time to time but was currently in Spain with her personal trainer. She took him everywhere with her so he was available whenever she felt the need to *work out*. Living on her trust fund, the slim red-haired young woman tried to remember the last time she saw her father alive. She couldn't.

Erin made an appearance at the funeral, of course, and later at the lawyer's office to see how long her monthly cash injections would continue. Even though he never showed it, daddy must have loved her; she was set for life. Telling the rest of the family she needed time to grieve, Erin said she'd spend time alone at the estate in Parrot Cay. In reality, it was her chance to hook up with the latest man in her life.

A colored sail appeared on the horizon, growing larger as the trade winds carried the craft closer to shore. She saw the pink and purple stripes of the mainsail, a customization she'd suggested after he bought the schooner, now that he had the means to do it.

Her manservant appeared with a fresh cocktail. He put a hand up to shield the sun and located what she was staring at. "Mr. Connors, I presume?"

52
Hunches

Lynda Campbell saw Abigail Brown heading back to her office with Ackley Scott in tow. She made it to the door just as they sat down.

Brown leaned back in her chair and eyed her friend. "Any ideas on how to track down Connors?"

"Sorry, no. I've got BOLOs out to the FBI and Interpol...maybe we'll get lucky...but..."

"But what?"

"Well, I know the captain likes Connors and thinks we'll wrap this whole thing up once we slap cuffs on him...but he doesn't feel right for this. An ex-cop with rich women falling all over him...why would he?"

Scott cut in. "I don't think I need to remind you ladies Henry Jensen was an ex-cop, and serial killer." He turned to Brown. "But I've noticed the murders have stopped since Connors disappeared... coincidence?"

Abigail shook her head. "I don't do coincidence...could be a hundred reasons the murders stopped. Plus, we have lots of other suspects looking good now that we have a description to go on. Gervais and Blanchard have two possibilities they're bringing in today, and I'm sure there'll be more once everyone gets on the same page."

Campbell's twisted face showed concern.

"What is it, Lynn?"

She was still standing in the doorway, leaning on the frame. "A hunch, I guess."

"Hunches and guesses are good..."

"That guy I told you about...that used to work for Delancey...Elmer Fudd..."

Brown's eyebrows popped and Scott laughed, "The cartoon character?"

Lynda laughed at herself. "Knudsen...that's what he called the guy and now I can't get the name out of my head. He was very bitter after losing his job at one of Delancey's pharmacies. He was being evicted from his family home, and blamed all his problems on the millionaire. I had a gut feeling the whole time we talked with him...he was definitely holding back on us."

"Does he match our suspect profile?"

"I'm not sure...every time I think about him, I picture Elmer Fudd with Bugs Bunny. I have his real name in my notes and want to have another go at him, but Knudsen's in court all day."

Ackley was working the keys on his lap top and cut in. "Elbert Fromm, I've got your report right here...nothing in police records other than your interview."

Lynda nodded. "Fromm...that's it. He was in pharmacy school and had to drop out when he lost his job. He couldn't pay his dead father's medical bills. There was an eviction notice on his door and he was in the process of moving out when we were there."

Abigail put her elbows on the desk and placed her chin in open palms. She stifled a yawn. "Sorry, didn't get much sleep last night. Sounds like you need to see Elmer Fudd again...maybe bring him in and turn up the heat."

Lynda yawned. "Now look what you've done. I agree. If he hasn't vacated yet...I think he was supposed to be out that day or the next. I'll see if one of the other guys can come with me."

Abigail was already on her feet. "No need. I'll come along...I'm only pushing paper around here and Ackley can cover for me." She glanced down at him and he nodded his approval.

"That would be great, Abs, I'll go get my stuff."

The two detectives crossed the war room and were almost to the door, when the Hun called out for one of them to come see her before leaving. Not sure what she wanted, they turned to each other and did rock, paper, scissors to see who would go. Campbell lost.

Abigail waited at the door for less than a minute. "That was quick."

"She gave me her lunch order."

53
Limelight

Bruce Dunn missed being in the limelight. He briefly made top dog in the office after taking out the drug dealer, and he had to find a way back to glory. After hearing how pissed off the captain was about Mike Connors disappearing, he decided finding the private dick would be his ticket back to the front row. He gave it careful thought, and asked himself who else besides law enforcement, could tip him off as to the missing suspect's whereabouts.

Deanna Delancey was the person to ask. Connors ripped her off, and if anyone had good reason to find him, it would be her. Being wealthy meant she was connected. By having those special friends, she might be able to point him in the right direction. He'd worked mostly solo since Cummings was off, and he took it upon himself to work his new angle alone.

As luck would have it, the widow Delancey was still in town, tidying up her late husband's estate. Dunn wondered if the poor bastard knew about her affair. He dug into the murder book and found the statement she gave during her interview. Her lawyer had done most of the talking so he called him. The mouthpiece was reluctant at first, but when he heard the detective's motives included the possible recovery of money, he was all in, and set up a meeting between his client and the detective.

Dunn was shocked when Deanna Delancey treated him like a long lost relative, even though their skin shades of ebony and ivory made that concept impossible. The widow wore a skin-tight silk dress, short and sheer enough that Dunn needed little imagination to picture her naked. It was low cut, showing an obviously expensive boob job. The short and stocky detective actually preferred them even bigger, with a matching plump booty.

When it became obvious that she'd had enough of his ogling, he asked if he could sit and get down to business. Delancey's lawyer had prepped her for his visit. She was anxious to hear him out, and told the detective to make himself comfortable. Dunn came right out with it. He believed Mike Connors was the Millionaire Murderer, and he wanted to take him down. He knew the widow was more interested in trying to recover her money, so he slanted the conversation that way. Dunn asked for details; her last movements with Connors...places they'd been together...where exactly she banked her money... and any associates he could question.

Deanna began by venting and name-calling, in an attempt to purge some of her ill feelings and frustrations toward her ex-lover. In letting her ramble on for what seemed like an eternity, Dunn wondered if the ice queen ever had any real feelings for Connors. It seemed as though he was only a means to an end. She used him as a pawn to topple the king or at least put a major dent in his bank account.

When she paused to take a breath, Dunn asked how she met Conners. He already knew some of the story but learned the former state cop was more than Lance Delancey's driver and bodyguard. She said he was also a fixer, who took care of certain things her husband never discussed. Connors openly admitted he was paid extra to watch her and had once given hush money to another woman who fell in love with Delancey, and wanted to break up his marriage.

She talked about their time in Florida. Connors rented boats from a friend, when they sailed to the Bahamas. It was on one of those excursions, they got the idea to park her nest egg into a Cayman Islands bank account. She'd gotten the bank connection from a girlfriend who was hiding money from her own husband.

The detective couldn't imagine ever having the amount of money she bitched about losing. To his surprise, she hinted it could be lucrative for him personally, if he was able to recover her stash. She scoffed and soured quickly when he informed her anything seized would be held by police as evidence. It was a murder investigation, after all.

The black widow also filled in the police detective about Connors' other affairs. One he already knew about with another victim's wife. When she mentioned the name of the young tart that he absconded with, Dunn's heart skipped a beat. She was half the PI's age and lived off her daddy's money. Deanna had done her own investigating, it seemed.

It was too much of a coincidence. Erin O'Reilly had to be the daughter of another millionaire murder victim. Dunn was sure that surname was on the hit list. His heart raced. He'd figured it out; the missing piece of the puzzle that could get him promoted. Connors chauffeured and did security for millionaires in the Detroit area. It was the illusive connection between the victims.

Dunn left the widow Delancey and headed downtown. He wondered if he should follow the chain of command and go to his old mentor, Lieutenant Harris, or bypass her and report directly to the man who really mattered, the captain. He was almost downtown when he remembered the cake.

Cummings had pulled the pin and he would be at the office for an impromptu retirement party.

Dunn checked his watch. He was late but figured it was payback for all the times his old partner fell asleep, or he had to wait on him. Cummings might have been a good cop in his day, but Dunn looked forward to getting a new partner. Someone to look up to him now that he solved the Millionaire Murders case.

54
Fudd

Campbell was behind the wheel, driving to 231 East Wisconsin Street. Her partner stared out the passenger window. "Delancey was killed in Highland Park…"

There was no reaction from Brown. "A glass of wine for your thoughts."

"Sorry, Lynn, you know how I get on a case like this. I can't help but think I'm in over my head…so many murders, a task force, and a shitload of information coming at me from all angles."

"You're too hard on yourself, Abs. It's the LT's job…looking after personnel, disseminating information to us, and keeping the brass in the loop. You have a lot of capable people working with you…let us do our jobs. You need to keep your eye on the big picture and have us focused on the end game. We're gonna get this guy."

Abigail wiped the corner of one eye with the tip of her finger. "I have my doubts…this one's different…everything he does is different. Those fucking mystery numbers…is he leaving clues and if so, why? If he wanted to get caught, leave evidence or a note, like other psychopaths who taunt police."

"Have your FBI cronies been any help to you?"

"More in guesswork than a concrete profile, and that only gets us so far…the proof is always in the evidence.

How many times have you heard that? Follow the evidence. Except in this case, there is no fucking evidence." Abigail's voice got louder as she spoke, her frustration showing.

"But we do have some evidence now...the forensics that gave you the suspect profile."

She tilted her head from side to side, as if contemplating Lynda's statement. "It's a start...but we still have to nail down a suspect, and find solid evidence connecting him to our victims. We're going to need a miracle on this one."

"Maybe we need to sit down with Simon again...or get him and Justin in the same room."

Abigail chuckled. "I suppose weirder shit has happened."

Lynda pointed up the street. "That should be our address, on the left. Looks like this used to be a nice neighborhood at one time." She pulled to the curb. "I see the eviction notice is still posted on the front door. Curtains are missing since the last time I was here. Maybe he finally moved out."

They made their way up the front walk and porch steps. Abigail grabbed a handful of mail from the letterbox and flipped through it. "Mostly junk mail...a couple pieces addressed to Elbert Fromm...an overdue utility bill." She knocked on the front door.

Lynda looked in the front picture window. "Looks pretty bare in there, and I don't see any movement."

Abigail tried the door handle but it wouldn't turn. "The key's broken off in the dead bolt." She shouldered the door and it popped open. "Guess it wasn't a good lock."

Lynda shrugged and followed her into the house.

They announced themselves and made their way through the empty rooms. There was nothing but more junk mail on the floor, along with discarded newspapers and magazines.

Noting the missing light fixtures, wall plates, and furnace grates, Campbell commented. "He really cleaned this place out." She wandered through the kitchen and checked the bedrooms.

Brown eyed the stacks of newspapers, wondering to herself who even read them anymore. She noted loose paper folded in one of the piles. They were single pages containing crossword and sudoku puzzles. Abigail leafed through them and saw every puzzle had been completed.

Lynda stopped at her side and looked past her shoulder. "What've you got there?"

"Seems Mr. Fudd likes crosswords and puzzles, and from what I can see here, he's very good at solving them."

"Hey...maybe he's your mystery man behind the newspaper Simon mentioned."

Abigail didn't reply. She stared across the room at nothing in particular.

"What is it, Abs?"

"Remember that gut feeling you had about this guy?"

"Yeah..."

"It's catchy...we need to find Elbert Fromm and have another chat with him. Do you have any other addresses we can check...maybe the last place he worked?"

"No, he didn't elaborate and nothing showed up in our files...he was clean."

Abigail kicked at another pile of newspapers. "Let's look through this stuff, just for shits and giggles. I'm gonna call Ackley and see if he can check local pharmacies to find out where he was employed."

"Sounds good...guess we don't need a warrant if he no longer lives here. Maybe you can ask Ackley to check the local colleges for pharmaceutical courses too?"

Abigail, already on the phone, nodded in agreement.

55
Meatloaf

The lineup at the soup kitchen is longer than usual. It gets this way when the temperature drops or it rains. The dog days of summer are cooler than normal and inclement weather sends the less fortunate for food and comfort indoors. For me, it means a home-cooked meal and a place to hide in plain sight. Fresh vegetables are on the menu. I wonder if my anonymous donation had anything to do with it.

It not that I don't have the money to eat in fancy restaurants every day; I was brought up to appreciate every dollar, and what it provided for my family. My mother wasn't a great cook, but I never went hungry. She tried to avoid things I disliked whenever she could. Not fussy by any means, I regard food as a necessity and not something to fuss over.

The mission is attached to a homeless shelter, where I keep a locker. It's supposed to be off limits to even the staff; a secure place to stash some of my murder money. Some might call it blood money but Delancey didn't bleed. Other victims donated to the cause too, but nothing close to the pot of gold the greedy pharmacy mogul offered me to live a few minutes longer.

I thank the server for the hot meal, and take my usual seat on the far side of the room; my back to the wall. It is the perfect place to take in the dining hall, and either ignore or wave off anyone who breaches my personal space. Silence is my only friend. I have no interest in anyone else at the mission, and they certainly don't need to know anything about me. Keeping quiet and staring off into space, usually keeps others at bay.

Street people are normally loners, who keep to themselves and don't bother anyone. That is the persona I take on. Just another guy down on his luck—certainly not a methodical serial killer on a personal quest.

A man of means is in the kitchen. He peels off the top half of his two-thousand-dollar suit, rolls up his sleeves, and slips on an apron. Even with the kitchen cloth on, his gold Rolex and gaudy rings scream rich bastard. They show up occasionally, spending an hour of their valuable time giving back to the community. If that is their goal, why don't they hand out thousand-dollar-bills to everyone in the room?

Seeing that wealthy businessman sparks the pilot light that has been lying dormant in my gut. I know the feeling—it is a flame within me and will burn until I do something about it. I do have mixed emotions. The feelings of remorse and guilt that came over me at the funeral still linger.

The meatloaf is very good, much better than the stuff mom made. Gravy was my savior back then, an aid to help wash down her best efforts. She tried so hard, and actually believed that I was crazy about her loaf, and the gravy was for my mashed potatoes.

I enjoy my meal and try to ignore the corporate executive. I wonder who he is, and just how I might go about killing the man.

56
Kangaroo

Detective Brown studied one of the puzzles she seized from Fromm's abandoned home. "Fuck me. I'm no dummy, but these number puzzles are way too complicated for me."

Campbell's eyes shifted, from the road, to Abigail, and back. "Maybe we need a specialist...like a mathematician."

"They solve equations and shit. There's something called numerology I've read about...where some believe there's a numerical value to the letters in words and names, or there's a mystical relationship between numbers and coinciding events."

"That sounds pretty deep. I hate to keep bringing this up, but isn't that what Simon was talking to you about?"

Abigail blew the contents of her lungs through puffed cheeks. "I don't know what to believe any more, Lynn. Perhaps he and Justin are onto something...a level of consciousness or understanding beyond mere mortals like me and you. I've been thinking all along the numbers are a clue but maybe our killer is a savant who's taken his own meaning from them. Either way, the guy who did these puzzles is no idiot."

"So, we're on the same page. Fromm is a good suspect... he's worth digging into deeper?"

Brown folded the newspapers and tucked them between the seats. "Yep. Deep like a well. A guy who worked as a pharmacist and solves puzzles like these has got some smarts...maybe even enough to keep us chasing our tails." She glanced at her watch. "I haven't heard back from Ackley. Let's head back to the station and find out what else is going on.

It was late in the afternoon when Detectives Brown and Campbell walked into the office. The bullpen was buzzing, unusual for that time of day. Lieutenant Harris spotted the female detectives and frantically waved them over like a traffic cop.

The Hun wore a sour expression, as if she just swallowed spoiled milk. Nearing their boss's door, Campbell fell in behind Brown to let her take the brunt of whatever was coming. Abigail caught it, slowed her pace, and caused Lynda to bump into her. She spoke out of the side of her mouth. "Chicken."

They stopped at the Hun's door. Harris appeared more disheveled than usual. Clumps of her hair stuck out in different directions, as if she tried to pull it out with both hands. Her lipstick was smeared, like she'd taken a right hook to the mouth.

Abigail stood fast. "You want to see us, LT?"

Harris craned her neck to see Campbell. "Soup, you got a valid passport?"

Brown stepped aside, leaving her friend in the line of fire. "What...yeah...why?"

"You and Dunn are going to Parrot Cay tomorrow."

Campbell's mouth fell open and it took a few seconds for the words to come out. "Where the heck is Parrot Cay, and why are we going there? Better yet, why is Dunn going with me...where's my partner?"

"It's an island in the Turks & Caicos...your man Connors is there. Your partner is still tied up in court. Dunn got it from a source down there, your killer is cruising the Caribbean on his new boat, and is holed up on a little island nobody's ever heard of."

Campbell turned to Brown, then snapped her head back to face the Hun. "Why the..."

The lieutenant put her hand up, once again the traffic cop. "Don't gimme no guff...this comes straight from Captain Kangaroo. Dunn convinced him Connors is our killer, and he's been given the green light to extradite his ass here. Since it's your case, I thought you should accompany him. And you're now on my shit list for forgetting my lunch."

Abigail cleared her throat and was about to speak, but she thought better. It was obvious the Hun was pissed, especially if she made fun of her own boss in front of them. She left Lynda with the lieutenant and headed across the room to see Ackley Scott. He smiled when she dropped into the chair beside his desk. "What the fuck has been going on in here since we left?"

Scott tilted his head toward the captain's office, where Dunn was sitting inside. The glass door was closed, but way the two were carrying on, it appeared they'd been best buddies forever. Ackley spoke in a hushed tone. "Dunn did some homework on his own, and apparently self-proclaimed himself a hero again, by tracking down Mike Connors."

"Why the hell is he so hyped on him...I thought he was cleared?"

"You'd have to ask him or the captain...or maybe the LT. I think she knows the whole story, but isn't buying into it. The two of them had a big blow up in his office—loud enough that I could hear parts of it. From what I gathered; he promised the mayor that we'd have his best friend's killer in custody by week's end."

Abigail shook her head, mulling over the turn of events. "Captain Kangaroo."

"What?"

"That's what the Hun called the captain...she's obviously pissed off. I guess Dunn's not *her* boy anymore...looks like he got a new mentor. Fuck 'em. Did you get a chance to look into Elmer Fudd?"

Ackley chuckled. "I like that name. No, sorry...I got sidetracked with the numbers and dates on our list. I had another look...trying to think like Justin and I searched newspaper archives."

"And...?"

"I found some of the dates are when particular company mergers or takeovers occurred."

"And like I said...how does that help us?"

His head on a swivel, Scott glanced around the room to make sure no one was within earshot. "The dates match the numbers."

She ogled him as if he had two heads. "You lost me."

Ackley smiled and leaned in closer. "Abigail, the mystery numbers represent how many people were fired or laid off as a result of the corporate actions on the dates Justin listed. I've been able to match them perfectly in four of our cases, so far. Newspaper articles referred to the numbers after mergers were announced." He frowned. "Like death notices in an obituary."

It hit her like a baseball bat to the forehead. She reached over the desk, grabbed Ackley's head, and kissed him on the lips.

57
Bulldog

Lynda Campbell told Bruce Dunn to meet her at the airport. It was easier for her to drive and park there instead of going downtown first. Spending three hours on an airplane with him and his ego would be enough for her. Her plan was to put her earbuds in when she arrived at the airport and ignore him for as long as she could.

She didn't dislike her fellow detective, but along with his swollen ego, Dunn was one of those men who thought he could do the job better than any woman. He was always polite and cordial to her, but never went out of his way to include her in any of his conversations or investigations.

She was briefed in the lieutenant's office, but he made sure to keep his cards close to his chest; saving any glory for himself. The Hun remained silent while Dunn put on his show, but Campbell saw her eyes roll at least twice during his performance. Harris informed the detectives the captain put through the expense claim, and they should attend the deputy chief's office before end of business, to pick up their airline tickets.

Campbell was back at her desk preparing for the trip when Knudsen checked in after finishing in court for the day. He was his usual jovial self, cracking off about the incompetent defense lawyer. It took a few minutes before he caught on to his partner's somber mood. When he asked what was up, she filled him in how Dunn had hijacked their case, replacing him. She and Dunn were flying south to arrest Connors.

Knudsen took a moment to wrap his head around what he just heard. He grabbed a stapler off Campbell's desk, and threw it across the room at Dunn. Luckily, the Bulldog had his head down and the projectile smashed against the wall behind him. The office went quiet. Everyone in the room stopped what they were doing and passed glances between the two men.

Dunn was startled and jumped from his chair, but a look across the room at the enraged gorilla who starred him down, kept him from responding.

Knudsen turned back to Campbell. "Sorry about the stapler. Guess I'm not needed here. I'm going home. My condolences on your new partner." On his way out, Square Head flipped Dunn the bird.

58
Broken

Abigail liked to be the first one in the office, especially when she was working a big case. She was surprised to find the Hun, busy at her desk. Harris had left the night before with her tail between her legs. That left only Brown and Scott working alone into the twilight hours. After settling into her chair and firing up her computer, Abigail checked phone messages and email. She took note of a call from Doug Cowper, telling her to check her mail.

Her forensic friend had secured more pieces of evidence to fit into their suspect profile. The FBI lab forwarded him DNA results, which identified European heritage, most likely Greek, with a history of heart disease. Cowper also had some luck with tire impressions and paint transfer from the O'Reilly hit and run. The vehicle was a Ford product produced between 2005 and 2008. The tire size indicated the vehicle was a pickup truck or van, possibly the F150, which was their best-selling vehicle and easiest to steal. Cowper apologized for assuming the truck or van was stolen, but no suspect vehicle had been recovered, and the killer was proficient in not leaving an evidence trail behind.

Abigail forwarded a copy of the forensic report to her file, and scrolled through it again. She used the additional information to form a picture of the suspect in her head, putting him behind the wheel of a Ford pickup...no...a Ford van. That made more sense, a commercial vehicle like a delivery van from a drug store. If the suspect was someone like Elbert Fromm, who once worked in a pharmacy, the mental image worked.

The detective was so absorbed in her work she didn't notice the lieutenant standing in her office doorway. Given her size, the Hun could never be invisible. She hadn't said a word to announce her presence, and Abigail missed the floor vibrations and heavy breathing; usual clues of her approach. "I'm sorry to disturb you, Detective, do you mind if we talk for a minute?"

Abigail thought about pinching the back of her hand to see if she was awake. Who was this woman in front of her? "Sure, LT, c'mon in and have a seat. What can I do for you?" She didn't know Jamila Harris that well; the woman hadn't been in the unit that long. The Hun had a good reputation for backing her people and getting the job done. She had her quirks but Brown had no reason to dislike her, and she respected the rank.

"I just wanted to say that I appreciate the hard work you and Detective Scott are doing on this investigation and the extra hours of your own time you've put in, even though you're not getting paid for them. I will make it up to the both of you, somehow, I promise."

She took a deep breath, as if to compose her next words carefully. "I'm so upset about what transpired yesterday, and I apologize for losing my cool in the captain's office. You've been here longer than I have and I think you have a pretty good handle on things. When it comes to investigators, Abigail, you're one of the best I've seen."

Brown blushed but accepted the compliment gracefully.

"But our captain is a different kind of animal...not only does he not have any investigative experience, he's an arrogant ass-kisser who has gone a few ranks higher than he ever should have. In short, the man's an idiot."

Abigail thought she should respond but wasn't sure how to and chose to nod her head in agreement.

Harris continued. "Having said that, he is still my boss, and yours, and we have to follow orders. The result is the useless trip to the Caribbean for Campbell and Dunn. He's another disappointment...I had high hopes for that kid. Anyway, I know you have your own thoughts on our serial killer and they don't include Mike Connors."

She paused so Abigail spoke up. "I do...we do, LT. It was Campbell's lead actually; a good suspect. Ackley and I have been working on it since Lynda's been taken out of the equation. His name is Elbert Fromm. He was interviewed by Campbell and Knudsen during their initial canvass. Lynda and I went to rattle his cage again but the bank foreclosed on his house, and he's disappeared."

The lieutenant sat back in her chair and crossed her arms. "Tell me why you like this guy."

Abigail filled her boss in about Fromm's bitterness over his father's death, and the unpaid medical bills that bankrupted him and knocked him out of school. Add the loss of his job, threats he made when he left, the experience he gained in a pharmacy, his uncanny ability to solve complex puzzles, and the fact he fit their suspect profile.

The Hun took it all in and nodded her approval.

The detective gave Harris the closer; how they finally figured out what the mystery numbers were and what they meant. What they would mean to someone like Fromm, a victim of a corporate raid by his former boss and millionaire, Lance Delancey.

The lieutenant dropped her hands to the arms of the chair and pursed her lips in thought. She hadn't blinked in a while and Abigail was afraid of what might come next. The Hun stood up. She glanced over her shoulder, in the direction of her boss's office. "We'll keep this to ourselves for now, and that goes for the comments about Captain Kangaroo. Let him and his new bum boy chase after the PI, and we'll watch it backfire when they are sued for false arrest.

I'm sorry Detective Campbell was caught in the middle. I know you two are close. Take Scott and any of the other investigators here you might need and see this thing through. Include Knudsen for sure. By the look of the dent in the wall, he's very pissed off. I can't say I blame him." She reached for the doorframe but stopped short. "Keep up the good work, Detective." The lieutenant turned and left Brown's office.

Brown was flabbergasted. Her impression of Jamila Harris was all wrong. The woman was a compassionate and inspirational leader who made no bones about having her back. She might not show it, but the lieutenant was a class act. Abigail watched her boss walk away. She had a completely different impression of the woman. Until the Hun grabbed the back of her slacks and pulled them out of the crack of her ass.

59
Hunting

I followed the Rolex man from the soup kitchen after lunch that day. They called him Mr. Segal when they thanked him for his generosity and donating his time. There was no bodyguard or driver waiting out front, where the rich dude parked his Mercedes sports coupe. He slid in behind the wheel and used the mirror to check his teeth and fix his hair.

There hadn't been anything in the news about company mergers or takeovers, and I was getting bored of doing puzzles. People watching, and imagining their life stories, was entertaining at times, but I needed more of a challenge; like hunting human prey. It became an addiction for me; tracking a person, and moving in for the kill.

I waited at the mouth of the alley that ran alongside the mission. The used Chrysler I borrowed from a huge auto mall owned by one of my victims blended in perfectly.

John Thomas was a self-made millionaire who started with one used car lot that did so well, he bought out his competitors, and turned the business into an empire. I drugged Thomas to help me get the big man into position for his electrocution. Like most of his wealthy cronies, he begged for mercy and offered me whatever I wanted. The man didn't keep much cash on hand, but his set of master keys for various car franchises was coming in quite handy.

As on previous occasions, I simply visited one of the parking lots late at night and helped myself to a vehicle in the back row. I always took one that was barely visible from the office up front. So far, I'd been able to borrow cars or trucks whenever I needed one.

It was a good system, better than the pharmacy van I used in the beginning. That was another situation where I forgot to return the keys. The vehicle wasn't missed when I used it at night and returned it by morning. To be safe and avoid detection, I thought it best to use different vehicles that were less identifiable.

I followed Segal to a high-end jewelry store on Woodward Avenue. After finding a good parking spot to conduct surveillance, I was surprised at how quickly my prey exited the store and returned to his car. The flashy sign above the entrance read, 'Pristine Jewelers'. It was too easy to make the connection. Segal's Mercedes sported a license plate that read, PRISTINE.

Knowing he visited the soup kitchen twice a week, I let Segal drive away. With the exception of an employee behind the counter, the store appeared empty. I got out of the car and walked across the street. There were two sets of glass doors at the entrance, with a buzzer to gain entry. The clerk eyeballed me as a potential customer, but given my casual clothes, probably wondered if I could afford anything in the store. A friendly smile and gentle wave got me buzzed in. Conversation was immediate when I didn't bother to look around.

I asked if Mr. Segal was in. He was supposed to meet me there about a job interview. The clerk offered a puzzled expression and said I just missed him. He said it was odd his boss sent me there, since applications were normally handled at the office in Farmington Hills.

I played dumb and apologized. I explained I may have been mistaken about the location, and would take a drive out there. The clerk seemed to feel bad about the mishap and offered me a business card with store locations, phone numbers, and an email address. He said there was an on-line application that would save me a lot of driving time. I thanked the helpful employee and left the store.

With my next victim's name, license plate, business, and a website to browse, I had no trouble filling in the blanks on my kill list. I wondered if it was worthwhile checking out the other stores. Why bother? Segal had more than one store and that meant plenty of employees. The big question was if the wealthy prick had wronged any of them and deserved to die.

60
Azure

Lynda Campbell was sure Bruce Dunn got the message. She was pissed at how he went behind her back and hijacked her investigation, and how he convinced the captain Mike Connors was the millionaire murderer, without any real proof. After her last conversation with Abigail Brown, she felt Elbert Fromm was their number one suspect. Their trip to apprehend the wayward private investigator was nothing but a wild horn-dog chase.

She listened to music and took in a movie on the flight to Miami. She sat by herself at an airport charging station, telling Dunn she needed to check in on her ailing mother. It wasn't until they landed on North Caicos Island and met an officer from the Coast Guard, that she paid any attention to her companion.

Dunn told her he didn't trust the Island Police and had made the connection with the Coast Guard through a friend in Detroit. They supplied Dunn with records of Connors' movement through the chain of Bahama and Cayman Islands, having tracked his GPS transponder beacon at the Dunn's request. Legally, Connors didn't have to check in at each port or island if he stayed within a particular country.

Campbell had been north to Canada and as far south as Florida, but she wasn't prepared for the beautiful colors of the Caribbean. The white sand was like baby powder, and the blue water was incredible. She'd seen pictures and always wanted to visit, but actually being there was thrilling. It was too bad they weren't staying long enough to enjoy it.

Parrot Cay is a private island off North Caicos. The Detroit Police Detectives visited the Royal Turks & Caicos Islands Police and commandeered a constable to accompany them to the O'Reilly estate. Even with extradition papers in hand, the desk sergeant was not impressed by the surprise visit. In the spirit of cooperation, he assigned one of his men to assist the arrogant American police.

They stopped at the end of a private laneway leading toward the beach. The oceanfront villa was not visible from their side of the large sand dunes. Dunn scoffed at the 'No Trespassing' sign and proceeded ahead. A white and blue stucco house came into view, its colors matching the surf and sand perfectly, almost camouflaging the beachfront mansion. The constable led the way to the front door and was about to knock, when the Bulldog broke off and worked his way around toward the back of the house.

There was no answer at the door. Campbell followed her partner's path around back and found him staring over a fence at a woman sunbathing in the nude, by the pool. The female detective called out to her, before Dunn was caught gawking and embarrassed himself. The young woman was startled and grabbed a robe to cover up. Campbell flashed her badge, apologized for the intrusion, and asked if she could meet them at the front door. Lynda turned and told her partner to put his tongue back in his mouth.

The constable was confused, as he was a few steps behind and had missed the show. He followed the American detectives back to the front door.

Dunn took the lead again, like a dog chasing its ball. He was way out of his jurisdiction but it didn't seem to concern him, and he only brought the constable because he had to. When the front door opened, Dunn charged past the young woman asking, "where is he...where's Connors?" and began searching the house. She immediately grew defensive, demanding to know who they were, and what they were doing there. The woman turned to follow Dunn but Campbell explained the reason for their visit, and asked for her name.

Erin O'Reilly introduced herself and wanted to know why they were looking for Michael. By offering his first name, Campbell deduced there was a personal connection between the young woman and Connors. She was probably his latest conquest in a line of rich women. The constable remained at the front door, while the female detective followed Miss O'Reilly into the kitchen. She poked her head around corners along the way, looking for Dunn.

"He's not here." O'Reilly nodded toward the empty dock. "Gone fishing for the day and I don't know when he'll be back. Why are you looking for him?"

Dunn magically appeared in the kitchen. "He's wanted for murder."

O'Reilly laughed. "Murder...you've got to be kidding. Michael would never harm another human being. He's the kindest man I know. You've wasted a trip down here."

"He's a serial killer, Miss O'Reilly...he's killed several millionaires in Detroit...including your father."

Campbell showed almost as much surprise as O'Reilly. She couldn't believe Dunn went so far as to share that with the victim's daughter, who was probably still grieving. The young woman's face grew red and Erin O'Reilly shot back. "My father was killed in a hit and run."

There was no time for Campbell to interject and Dunn continued. "It was a hit and run but Connors did it and he's on the run...that's why he's down here with you, living off another woman's blood money."

Erin tried to speak but couldn't find the words. Dunn was proud as a peacock doing it's mating dance. He used his wild imagination to carry on and told the grief-stricken young woman everything he knew about the case. Campbell glanced at the constable who'd joined them in the kitchen. His dark brown eyes had grown as big as ripe chestnuts.

Tears streamed down O'Reilly's face and she stuttered while making excuses for her lover. Her legs shook and she reached to the counter for support. Campbell took her by the arm before she collapsed, and led her to a chair. The young woman shook her head, refusing to believe Michael had anything to do with her father's death, or anyone else's for that matter.

Dunn was relentless and demanded to know where Conners was and when he'd be back. Dunn claimed Connors would be arrested for multiple murders, and extradited to the United States. The young woman broke down, but it didn't deter the dogged detective. He said he couldn't find any of Connors' belongings in the house and asked if she was in on planning her father's death with him.

Nobody saw it coming. O'Reilly scooped a gin bottle off the table and flung it at Dunn. His quick reflexes saved him from a direct hit but the bottle careened off his shoulder, clipped his ear, and smashed against the wall. He took a step back and Campbell saw it as their cue to leave. She grabbed the Bulldog by the arm and said it was time to go.

The three cops regrouped in the car and Dunn went on about how he believed O'Reilly was probably in on it, and she was protecting Connors.

Campbell blew a gasket and laid in on him, telling him he was nothing but a bully. That he had no evidence of that fact, his whole investigation was a sham, and he was only trying to prove it so he could suck up to the captain. She said the real killer was back in Detroit, where they should be working on tracking him down.

Dunn pouted and sulked for a while. He got on the phone to someone and asked that they track Conners' boat again. The conversation was short. He announced there was no signal for the GPS transponder, and it either was off or disconnected. He gave Campbell a dirty look. "Are you happy now? Conners has disappeared again, and I have to go home empty handed."

61
Fromm

Whether Dunn and the captain believed it or not, Mike Connors was out of the picture as far as Abigail was concerned. He had been eliminated as a suspect long ago. The detectives in the office were chasing down leads on other potential suspects, to check them off their list, as is required in any homicide investigation. It's too easy to get tunnel vision when focused on the person believed to be responsible. That mistake can put innocent men in jail for crimes they didn't commit.

Brown and Scott believed Elbert Fromm was their man. Everything they dug up so far, pointed in his direction. Their next step was to get the man into the box for interrogation. They had to find him first. Their efforts the day before, a twelve-hour marathon, proved fruitless. Ackley searched the internet, while Abigail called pharmacies across the city, looking for anything on Fromm.

It was another day and Abigail was already into her second cup of coffee, trying to keep up the pace. There hadn't been a millionaire murder in weeks but it didn't mean one couldn't occur at any time. No one knew the killer's agenda. If they pinned him down somewhere, they might consider conducting surveillance to get a better idea of his movements or game plan. It was all guesswork at this point.

Ackley walked into Abigail's office with two fresh Danish from the diner across the street. "I thought you might like one to keep your sugar level up...to go with the caffeine."

She accepted the treat and put it to her nose. "Mmm...it's still warm...where'd you get these?"

"Across the street...Debbie's got fresh baked goods now."

"You still hoping she switches teams?"

Ackley blushed, but it wasn't from what Abigail said. Martha Wells just walked past her door and bent over an empty desk to answer a telephone. Abigail craned her neck to see why Scott was gawking. "Oh...she's single you know. Why don't you ask her out?"

He sat in the chair in front of her desk and sighed. "A bit out of my league."

"You won't know if you don't ask, partner. Besides, I've seen her checking you out when you're not looking."

"Right."

"Well, maybe not. But I do know her last boyfriend was a jock and she tired quickly of his macho attitude and coming second to his team."

"And how would you know that?"

"Girl talk...in the coffee room."

"Since when have you been one of the girls, or ever drank the office coffee?"

Abigail stuffed the Danish into her mouth and shrugged.

Scott chose to speak while his partner's mouth was full. "Any luck with our boy at the drug stores?"

She shook her head and quickly took another bite, as if she was afraid someone would take it away from her.

"Everything I found on line put him at the address you and Lynda checked out. He seems to have dropped off the grid after that. But get this...he has an online presence in one of the game rooms Justin and I play in. By the level of his expertise and avatar, it has to be him."

Abigail was still chewing on her Danish and using coffee to wash it down. She lifted her chin for him to continue.

"He goes by 'Cruciverbalist'. Fitting, I'd say."

She moved the half-chewed dough to one side of her mouth to speak. "What the hell is a Cruciverbalist? This Danish is awesome." She ate some more.

"Someone who solves puzzles or riddles. Most people have never even heard of the word."

"Including me, who makes up that shit? Can you track him somehow...through the site or by his IP address?"

"Tried that. He hasn't been online since his eviction...another reason I'm sure it's him. I'm keeping an eye on it. Justin has beaten him on number puzzles a few times but you've met him—he's not one to chat in person, let alone online. If Fromm signs back on, I'll try to figure out a way to converse with him."

Abigail licked her fingers and dabbed the corners of her mouth with a napkin. "Damn, that was good. Oh yeah, forgot to tell you...Smith and Jones found three pharmacies with Ford delivery vans that match our suspect vehicle. I told them you and I would check them out while they head up to Ann Arbor to visit the college where Fromm took his pharmacy course."

"Who are Smith and Jones, exactly?"

"The two guys from robbery, I can never remember their real names."

"You sound like the Hun."

"She named them...something about a TV series called 'Alias Smith & Jones'."

Ackley wrapped up his Danish after only a few bites. "I remember that show as a kid...it was a western and they were cowboys."

"They fit the bill, I guess." She eyed his Danish. "You gonna finish that?"

He pulled it from her reach and held it close. "I don't know how you eat like that and keep your figure."

Abigail grinned. "Thanks for noticing. Running five miles a day helps. Give me about an hour to finish up some paperwork here, and we'll take a ride and check out those drug stores."

"You sure it's alright to take me out on the road with you?"

She shrugged. "The Hun doesn't seem to mind, and I promise to keep you out of trouble. If Fromm is as smart as we think he is, we probably won't run into him." She paused in thought for a few seconds. "He doesn't really scare me...he appears to be focused on millionaires and seeks out weapons of opportunity to do the deed. He doesn't seem like the type to keep strapped...just saying."

Scott turned to leave her office but stopped at the door. "You hear anything from Lynda?"

"Yeah." Abigail rolled her eyes. "They missed Conners and he's still in the wind. Lynda's pissed at Dunn. She left him at the hotel and went out for the night with a young constable she met there. Our detectives are supposed to be heading home later this afternoon. I haven't seen the captain around at all today...he's probably hiding out or booked off sick so he can avoid the mayor."

Ackley shook his head. "Come and get me when you're ready to go."

62
Bored

Surveillance is boring. Sitting in a car and watching Neil Segal at work is comparable to watching paint dry. I breeze through a book of crossword puzzles...nothing better to do. I'm happy to have a name to go with the face.

Online research on my future victim proves more difficult than most, the wealthy jeweler has no public persona and keeps his business dealings confidential. From what I discovered so far, Segal has several high-end stores scattered across Michigan, and a chain of pawnshops near casinos in three different states. It's my educated guess the success of one led to the other. It is no secret half the jewelry they take in off the street is stolen. Resetting stones and melting down precious metals is common in the industry. After Segal's craftsmen work their magic on someone's stolen heirloom, the shiny new replacement is completely unrecognizable. The profit margin is huge.

That sticks in my craw. My father gave me permission to pawn some of mom's jewelry to help pay debts, but by the time I raised enough cash to get the items back, they'd been sold. I suspect that was bullshit, and that the pawnshop belongs to Segal. My mother's jewels were no doubt reconstituted, and sold to some stranger. What kind of asshole can do something like that? Does he not have a conscious or make enough money on new product? It is no wonder people hate Jews.

A burning sensation grew in the pit of my stomach. It's a familiar feeling I get when someone makes my hit list. Is Segal as bad as the others? He is ripping people off but he hasn't taken their livelihood away like Delancey, and the other rich bastards did. Maybe all wealthy people are the same; building their empires by taking advantage of others...people down and out like me and my father.

I glance at the dashboard clock and flip the page to start a new crossword. It is almost quitting time for Segal. I already know where the jeweler lives, but want to confirm a timeline for his daily movements. There always seems to be someone else in the family home, so the location for his demise will probably have to be somewhere else. Burned was the answer to number one across. I laughed. In keeping with my repertoire of methods to kill, I consider what I can do with a smelter. Maybe, Segal can be melted down like a piece of precious metal, and turned into something uglier than he already is.

I'm half-way through the puzzle when my prey leaves the store. Segal makes two stops and drives towards home. Checking the clock again, I figure dinner is being served at the soup kitchen. I made the next left to head in that direction. The spot in the alley where I like to stash my ride is vacant so I park.

Pangs of hunger steal my thoughts and I pay little attention to the others in the dining hall. It's a mistake that puts me in an awkward position. Nearing the kitchen counter, I see a well-dressed man and woman talking to the padre who runs the mission...cops. The tall black female glances in my direction just as the mashed potatoes hit my plate. I let the weight of the food pull the tray from my hands and watch as it falls to the floor.

Taking a knee to clean up the mess, I notice the cop's attention is back on the padre. The distraction keeps me out of their direct line of sight. Turning my back, I dump the spilled meal in the garbage. Feigning I'm going to clean up, I head for the washroom. Past the men's room there is another door that leads to the alley. I don't look back and make my exit.

63
Leads

Detectives Brown and Scott visited the first pharmacy on their list of stores that used a Ford van for deliveries. They waited five minutes for the busy clerk to get off the phone, only to refer them to the assistant manager who was due back from lunch at any time.

Abigail turned to Ackley. "Got any shopping to do while we wait?"

He shrugged and wandered off toward the front of the store.

Abigail took the empty chair beside the prescription counter and thumbed through the texts on her phone, checking to see if she missed anything important. It was normal for her to ignore calls and messages when she was focused on a case.

She was leafing through a pamphlet advertising a new miracle drug for obesity, when a dark-haired East Indian man brushed past her and went behind the prescription counter. Brown stood up and watched the clerk point her out to him. The man approached the counter and asked how he could help. He spoke English but Abigail could barely understand his thick accent.

When the detective mentioned the Ford van, the assistant manager said the vehicle had been wrecked only a week before and was taken to the junk yard. She asked him about a former employee named Elbert Fromm and if he would have had access to the van when he worked there. The young man said he'd only been there a month and was unaware of such a person. He glanced at the female clerk but she shrugged and shook her head. Not ready to give up, Brown asked if they had records of their former employees or if there was someone she could talk to, who'd been there longer. She wasn't surprised by the response. Nobody knew Fromm and their personnel records were private information and couldn't be released without a warrant.

Ackley stepped up beside his partner. He informed the man patient information was privileged, but not employee records. He took offense at being challenged, and said they'd have to take it up with the manager, who was not in. Before her partner got himself worked up, Abigail grabbed him by the arm and led him away.

Back in their car, she flipped through Fromm's file. "I can't believe this is all we have on the guy. Who the hell doesn't have a valid driver's license these days? Didn't the pharmacies check on that? According to the date on the photo, this must have been his original license...and that was fifteen years ago. Fuck. How are we supposed to find the man when we don't even know what he looks like?" She looked at the sketch created from Lynda Campbell's description. "And this doesn't help much either...I know a dozen cops that look like this shitty sketch."

"As much as he's been online, using an avatar for gaming, he hasn't left much of a digital footprint. When I checked school records, he was never there for any of the class photographs. Maybe the cowboys will come up with something."

"Who?"

"The Smith and Jones characters, from robbery."

"That would be nice...but chances are he's not in any of their class photos either."

"Maybe we should be checking drug stores for security video...most have a camera behind the counter to keep an eye on their employees."

Abigail smacked Ackley's upper arm with the back of her hand. "That's a good idea, partner, I knew I kept you around for a reason."

"Don't get your hopes up too high...although most stores record digitally now, some only keep it for thirty days. But maybe we'll get lucky."

The next drug store was on Eureka near Toledo Road. Abigail found a parking spot down the block. There was an abundance of staff behind the counter in the pharmacy section; an older female clerk asked how she could help. The detectives produced their badges and ID cards, and asked for the manager.

The woman poked her head into a doorway and called to someone inside. A dark-skinned, grey-haired man in his sixties came to the counter and invited the police into his office. They all squeezed into the tiny room. The detectives remained standing because a stack of boxes filled the only chair. The manager apologized for the mess and asked how he could help.

Scott produced the images of Fromm while Brown questioned the man. He studied the photo and sketch and said he knew of the guy, but that the images were a poor likeness. Although the manager said he knew who Fromm was, he said he didn't see him much. He further explained how he was semi-retired and only worked at the store three days a week. He said Fromm was only there part-time too, while he attended school.

Scott asked if the store kept security video from behind the counter and the manager said they did, but only for a month. Seeing disappointment on their faces, the pharmacist asked what exactly it was that Fromm had done. Brown told him he was wanted for questioning in regards to a criminal investigation but that she couldn't elaborate.

The man nodded and asked if there was anything else he could do for them. Ackley asked if they used a Ford Econoline van for deliveries. The man said they did but it was currently out dropping off prescriptions. When asked if Fromm had access to the vehicle, the manager said his duties didn't include making deliveries, but the staff used the van for other reasons from time to time. The keys hung on a hook near the back door.

Climbing back in the car, Abigail commented they were 0 for 2 and she felt they were about to strike out.

Ackley replied. "You won't know until you take your turn at bat. The next store is on Warren Avenue, the other side of the Eastern Market. I'll tell you what...if we strike out there, I'll buy you dinner at your favorite deli."

"Ooh, big spender. And what do I get if we hit pay dirt?"

"A rain check, obviously, since we'll be working overtime, again."

The third store was also a bust so Abigail pointed the car toward the deli. The place was about to close but upon recognizing one of their favorite customers, the smiling little man in the apron waved them up to the counter. She ordered a Rueben with a side of dill pickles. Scott ordered the Montreal smoked meat with a cup of potato salad. Abigail opened her bag and stuffed her nose inside. "I'm glad we're close to work...this is going to be hard to leave alone until we get there.

Brown ate all the pickles, and fingered the loose meat, as they walked through the office door. She ripped open her bag and one corner of the sandwich was already in Abigail's mouth before she sat down behind her desk. She popped open the can of diet Pepsi the deli threw in on the house.

There was a note on her desk from Smith and Jones. It had a picture attached. The half-eaten sandwich fell from her hand, plopping on the desk. Abigail grabbed her purse and car keys and ran out. She yelled to Ackley, "Let's go...I know where he is!"

He asked if he should bring his sandwich, but his partner was already out the door. Barely making it through the closing elevator doors, Ackley asked, "Where who is?"

"Fromm." She handed him the photograph Smith and Jones had left for her. "He's at the mission...the guy who dropped his tray in the food line. Fucking sonofabitch was right there in front of us."

64
Spotted

Lynda Campbell went from the airport directly to the police station to see what was going on with the investigation into Fromm. She left the case in capable hands, but no one answered the phone in the office. Her attempts to reach Abigail went straight to voicemail. A call to her own partner, Knudsen, found him half in the bag at a local bar, where he was drowning his sorrows after losing his case in court.

He bitched and moaned but eventually got around to asking if she did him a favor and pushed Dunn overboard, feeding him to the fish. Campbell realized just how drunk her partner was when he changed the topic and asked if she did any nude sunbathing. It was a line he'd never before breached with her; then again, she never had a conversation with him when he was drunk.

Knudsen said he was pissed about his case and never bothered to check in at the office after court. He got mushy, apologized, and told her how much he enjoyed working with her. When he mentioned Dunn's name again, she cut him off and said she left the Bulldog at the airport, where a friend was supposed to pick him up. To keep her partner from rambling she told him how Connors was still in the wind and the captain had wasted her time.

After Knudsen promised to take a cab home, Campbell said she'd see him at the office, first thing in the morning.

She parked the company ride in the garage. When the elevator doors opened, she nearly bumped into Jamila Harris.

The lieutenant shook her head. "Sorry for the wild goose chase, Soup, looks like you got a bit of sun though...hope you had a Pina-colada for me. Where's the little dick head?"

"He had someone pick him up at the airport...I think he's trying to avoid the captain and everyone else in the office who wrote Connors off before we went on our little trip. Any idea what's going on with our suspect, Elbert Fromm?"

"Brown and Scott have been working on him...they believe he's our man and have been running down leads. I wanted to get an update before I left for the day but Crunch charged out of here like her ass was on fire. I was in the bathroom. Hacker ran after her, trying to catch up. Maybe give her a call...I gotta pick up dinner for my man."

"I tried...my calls keep going to her voicemail."

The Hun called over her shoulder as she walked away. "Try her partner..."

Campbell bypassed her own desk and went into Abigail's office. What was left of a corned beef sandwich lay in the middle of her desk; meat and sauerkraut were splattered across a note from two other detectives who checked out Fromm's Ann Arbor school. It said they got a positive ID on Fromm and brought back a recent photograph taken at the college. She picked up one of the copies. The image of the man she interviewed in his home came back to her. She was embarrassed the description she supplied the sketch artist barely resembled Fromm.

Campbell picked up Abigail's phone to call Scott. "Ackley...it's Lynda, where are you guys? I've been trying to reach..." She heard Abigail call out to him.

"We're at the downtown mission...Fromm was here. I gotta go..."

"What...?" Scott hung up.

The mission wasn't too far from the cop shop so Campbell got back in the car and drove over there. A well-weathered street person was on the way out the front door when she reached for the handle. The man's eyes averted hers and he slipped into his netherworld. Another homeless-looking man was busy doing dishes in the kitchen.

Campbell asked if he saw two police detectives or the person in charge of the place. He nodded toward a door to her right. She walked down a short hall and heard familiar voices coming from an open door. Campbell stuck her head in and saw her fellow detectives talking to a padre, in front of a row of storage lockers.

Abigail turned. "Lynda, what are you doing here?"

Campbell hesitated for a second, thinking it was her case, and she didn't need permission to be there. But this was Abigail, a more than capable detective she left in charge of the case while she was on her wild goose chase. "I just got back in town and wanted to catch up...tried calling you a few times but..."

"Sorry, Lynn, I've been ignoring my phone. Fromm was here today...we saw him in the bread line. He dropped his tray to avoid detection, slipped out the back door, and hasn't come back. We're just going through his locker."

"Don't we need a warrant?"

Abigail shook her head. She and Ackley were looking through several parcels of wrapped newspapers. "No expectation of privacy here...the locker belongs to the mission and they can search for weapons and such anytime. They do it when they feel the need. You can imagine what some street urchins might keep in here."

"What's in the paper?"

"It's how he stores and hides stuff." Abigail tilted her head toward a table with several unwrapped items. "He uses the crossword pages when he's done with them. His social security card is here, along with two grand in cash, some personal items, and a key to another storage locker."

"Does he sleep here at night?"

"The padre says our man only comes in for meals...and get this...he thinks Fromm made an anonymous cash donation to the mission."

"How would he know that?"

"He saw us unwrap the package of new one-hundred-dollar bills with sequential serial numbers. The padre said the donation came in the same way...go figure...our man has wads of cash to give away and he's eating with the homeless."

Lynda scoffed. "Who does he think he is, Robin Hood?"

Ackley spoke up. "Robin Hood didn't kill the rich after he stole from them. Maybe he's using the cash for fleabag motels and eating here to stay off the grid...would explain why there's no paper or electronic trail."

Abigail pursed her lips. "This guy is one of a kind...a mystery man on a mission...who has a big lead on us. We're slowly catching up though...a few steps at a time. He hasn't killed in a while. Fromm's either been studying someone new, or we've got him on the run, and he's hunkering down to look over his shoulder. Let's pack this stuff up and regroup at the office. I think I left my sandwich there."

Campbell laughed. "Maybe we should order a pizza...I cleaned up what was left of your Rueben. It was splattered all over your paperwork and the note with Fromm's photo. By the way...who are Smith and Jones?"

65
Googled

The change in season brings shorter days. The early dusk allows me to stand in the shadows, unnoticed. The same two cops, and another female detective, leave the soup kitchen. The light over the front door puts them on display for a few seconds. The tall black female is very becoming. The male cop is carrying an evidence bag that appears to hold the contents of my storage locker.

No doubt, the padre and all the staff will now be on the lookout for me. How sad...no more meatloaf on Mondays. Their split pea soup always brought back warm memories of my mother's rendition. Especially when she baked fresh bread to go with it...sourdough...I love the fluffy white stuff. The thought of food and how close I came to being discovered leaves an uneasy hollowness in my stomach.

I just lost a chunk of cash but there is more hidden elsewhere. The pair of detectives make a U-turn right in front of me. I go deeper into the shadows, but get a good look at the female cop. She is way too hot to be five-O. The other female investigator drives off in the opposite direction. Stepping into the evening gloom, I head for my borrowed car.

White Castle is the first fast food joint I come across so I grab a bag of cheeseburgers and chow down in a back corner of the parking lot. A cop car slips through the drive through without a glance in my direction. Dinner is their priority. I wonder how the female detective knows what I look like, and if my photo circulating throughout the department.

There was nothing in the locker that could hurt me, although my social security card would confirm my identity. I can't remember why I left it there. It was a stupid mistake I can't afford. For a guy who never thought the cops would catch him, I am getting sloppy and have to clean up my act. The key can be another problem.

It's for a post office box, not too far from the mission, my next stop after dinner. Then I will change vehicles again. It is best not to get comfortable, even though the Chrysler 300 I currently drive is a nice ride...a lot better than my shitty old Toyota. I can't believe the bank took it. What can they do with a piece of crap like that?

Not sure what photograph the cops might have, I pull a hood over my head and keep my eyes to the ground as I clean out the PO Box. Why give them new video images to use against me? I told the clerk my key was lost and I had to pay them fifty bucks to open the box. Not having any smaller bills to pay their ridiculous fee, I use one of the new hundreds from the stash in my sock.

Sorting through my stuff in the car, I think about the sequential serial numbers on the paper money. It is a trail I don't want to leave. The cash was from Delancey's secret stash, and I doubt the cops can use any of it to tie me to his murder. The problem is it's difficult to cash one-hundred-dollar bills anywhere other than a bank, where cameras and paperwork are problematic.

After selecting a slightly used Chevy Malibu, I head for the public library. The older branch in Mexican Town is perfect and they stay open until 10pm. It has private booths where prying eyes can't see what I'm doing. Patrons use the internet for free, but with a time limit of one hour. I never have a problem there late at night...the sketchy neighborhood keeps people at home. Before checking into my favorite game room, I search the Detroit Police website, looking for the attractive female detective from the mission. No luck there so I try googling DPD homicide dicks. Finally, I see the tall and lanky black bitch in a newspaper article. She is standing at the edge of the Detroit River, as police boats search for bodies.

Her name is Abigail Brown and she was the lead detective in a serial killer investigation where several women's bodies were recovered. Subsequent articles followed the investigation to the point where Brown shot and killed the suspect, a former Mountie from Canada. Impressive, to say the least.

I Google Brown and find other articles on her police exploits...one where she took down another serial killer. It seems the woman is a specialist of sorts. There is also mention of a partner being shot, and another partner killed by a fleeing felon. This bitch is the real deal. I keep digging but she doesn't have a profile on any mainstream social media sites.

An old picture pops up of her as a university basketball star. There is another of her in military uniform. I find an obituary for a man I think was her father. He was also a copper and killed in the line of duty. Wow, death seems to follow this chick. I flip back to the image of her standing by the river. She is so focused. Who is this cop and should I be worried about her?

The sudden police interest in me messes up my planned surveillance of Neil Segal...buying the wealthy jeweler more time to live. Watching him interact with his employees only reinforces my conviction that the man is like all my other victims; someone who only cares about himself and how much of a fortune he can accumulate.

I lean back in the chair and think about it. Instinctively, I swivel my head to take in the surroundings. There is no one else there except the librarian. Whenever I glance over, she makes a point of checking the clock. The bookworm obviously has somewhere else she would rather be and wants to close up so she can get there.

With another twenty minutes to go, I ignore her and log into the game room to check my ongoing games, and where I stand in the rankings. There isn't much competition at my level, except for one kid who sometimes matches my scores. Someone who uses the Jason mask from Friday the 13th as his avatar…a psycho with a high IQ, no doubt.

66
Team

Almost every detective was in the office before their shift officially started. It showed their dedication and determination to solve the millionaire murders case. Bruce Dunn was the holdout. He booked off sick, saying he picked up a bug down south. The captain hadn't been around in days. He left a phone message for Harris saying he'd be in budget meetings the rest of the week.

The war room buzzed with discussions over the tidbits of information available about their chief murder suspect, Elbert Fromm. Detectives hovered around the coffee table at the back of the room.

The Hun ordered in a large coffee urn and selection of bagels, donuts and muffins from the Tim Horton's located about ten blocks from the cop shop. She came out of her office with a coffee in hand, and her tongue working at a wad of fresh dough stuck in the back corner of her mouth. She thanked everyone for their tireless efforts so far, and asked for their continued diligence in what she believed, was the home stretch. With that remark, she turned to Abigail Brown to take over.

As lead detective on this sensational case, Brown looked the part. She stood erect as a flagstaff, and spoke with a tone resonating her experience and expertise. Although the seasoned detective always dressed well, her neatly pressed pantsuit and wide collared blouse looked fresh off the rack, and gave the impression she was the best-dressed person in the room. "I'd like to reiterate the lieutenant's comment about the excellent work everyone's done on this case. I agree we're in the home stretch on this thing. It hasn't been easy going, chasing after a killer without the usual evidence or leads to chase. Thanks to old-fashioned police work, we now know the millionaire murderer's identity.

"Having said that, we still have much to do in finding this killer, and building a case that will hold up in court. You've all heard his name, Elbert Fromm. He's smart and by all accounts, not your typical serial killer. He's made some mistakes along the way...little mistakes... the kind that will eventually lead to his capture. I'm sure of it."

Karl Knudsen asked, "What do you want us to do...to catch this bastard?"

Abigail smiled. "I like your enthusiasm...I'm getting to exactly that." That was Ackley Scott's queue to hand out assignments. "Detective Scott has something for each and every one of you...we all have rolls to play. Some bigger than others, but if we all do our part, we just might be able to net Fromm in the next couple days."

She used the whiteboard to lay out the master plan, showing all the points of surveillance; places Fromm was believed to frequent. Brown did a geographic profile of places he visited or was spotted, pinning down a three-mile area. She highlighted soup kitchens, pharmacies, newspaper stands, bookstores, and internet cafes. The profile was based on proven theory. Criminals tend to operate within their own comfort zones.

The noise level in the room picked up as the investigators read their assignments and discussed them with their partners.

Proud to see her team in action, the Hun nodded her approval to Abigail. She broke off and headed back to the dessert table. Like a kid at the candy counter, the lieutenant filled a small plate with donut holes. Astonishing the person next to her, she said they weren't as filling as the rest of the pastry.

Abigail Brown watched worker bees buzz around the room, gathering their thoughts before leaving the hive to fetch nectar for their queen. She never considered herself anyone's boss, even though she'd been told on more than one occasion she was supervisory material. As much as she enjoyed being in charge, Abigail craved action, and would wither and die if confined to a desk.

Being the lead investigator came with a lot of responsibility. They were the first to be blamed if something went wrong. Being in that position gave her the opportunity to see things through and ensure the investigation was conducted properly. Her actions indicated a good leader. Unlike a certain captain, who made emotional decisions based on peer pressure. Even with her quirks and eccentricities, the troops respected Brown.

Ackley Scott was waiting in Abigail's office when she returned to her desk with her third coffee of the day. "What, no more apple fritter's back there?"

She tried to cool the hot brew with a light blow, and took a sip. "One was enough for now...I missed my run this morning."

"That's not like you."

"It's your fault. After you called and told me about Fromm logging in at the library in Mexican Town, all I could do was work on a game plan in my head. It's a woman thing...not being able to shut off our brains."

"And you thought about that all night?"

"Well...no. There's other stuff to think about...like what to wear, is it clean or ironed, what shoes—depending on the weather, did I put the garbage out or lock the door, what would I eat for breakfast, if I'd have time for a run...important things like that."

Ackley gazed over the lid of his laptop. "Wow, I'm surprised you get any sleep at all. I'm OCD but pride myself on the fact I can go from my bed to my car in under forty minutes...and that includes a shit, shave and shower."

"Potty mouth...that's my forte."

"It just doesn't sound as good if you say poop. Anyway...I see you put Campbell and Knudsen on the library. What are we gonna do?"

"Sit tight for a bit. Lynda's going to slip into the library when it opens and see if she can check the search history on the computer Fromm used. I told her to give you a call so you can dig into whatever he was playing with online. See if we can predict his next move or pin down his next location. She is also gonna check if the key we found fits a post office box in the area."

"And you?"

"I'm going to double back on some of my calls and interviews. I want to see if I can fine-tune the geographic profile some more. A three-mile radius in the city covers too much ground. Something else is gnawing at me...how is Fromm getting around if he's not using the drug store van anymore? Maybe you can check the police reports for me before Lynda calls. See if any parked vehicles stand out."

"You got it, partner." Ackley stood up and reached over to Abigail's desk, opening a candy dish where she kept her sweets stashed. "Busted." He grabbed one of the Timbits and left her office.

She called out after him. "I forgot they were in there."

"Right. A bit less sugar and caffeine and you'll sleep just fine."

67
Building

Abigail was thumbing through her interview notes when the Hun called. The detective kept reading while she picked up. "LT, what can I do for you?"

"Can you come see me and the ADA in my office? He was tied up on another case and missed the briefing."

"No sweat, I'll be right there." Abigail sipped her coffee and read her notes while she walked to the lieutenant's office. Multitasking was her specialty. Her peripheral vision caught her partner ogling his favorite secretary. Brown wondered if she should pull Martha Wells aside and put in a good word for Scott.

She recognized the Assistant District Attorney from a previous court case where they worked together. Dale Walker was rumored to be the heir apparent to the existing DA...the retirement announcement was expected prior to the next election. His possible promotion was the reason Walker had been assigned to the high-profile murder investigation. A conviction in such a case would all but guarantee his advancement.

The ADA extended his hand to Abigail when she stepped into the lieutenant's office. Walker was a good prosecutor and a true professional who respected Brown for her accomplishments. He apologized for his tardiness, and motioned to the empty seat beside him, in front of Harris' desk.

"I'm glad we have a chance to talk alone." He glanced at the Hun's office door. Abigail got up and closed it. "I have to ask what direction your investigation is taking at this point...our office recently issued an arrest warrant and extradition order for Mike Connors, and now I'm hearing you have another suspect, and Connors is in the wind?"

Abigail opened her mouth to speak but Lieutenant Harris cut her off. "I take full responsibility for that caper, although the order to pursue him came from above."

Walker cleared his throat. "Don't get me wrong, ladies, I'm not on a witch hunt here. I know your captain, my boss, and the governor are all country club cronies. I accept some responsibility. I should have kept a closer eye on this investigation from the start. Politics should have nothing to do with it, but we all know how that works. So, bring me up to speed, please?"

The Hun nodded to Brown.

Abigail replied. "Connors is not a serious contender, but we still have people working to eliminate him as a suspect once and for all. We believe Elbert Fromm is our killer. He's made mistakes. Besides his name, we have a photograph confirming his identity. We also have forensic evidence collected from some of the crime scenes..."

Walker interjected. "But do you have enough for me to issue a warrant and make a case yet?"

The two women exchanged looks and Abigail continued. "Maybe, but it's mostly circumstantial at this point."

The ADA turned sideways in his chair to face Detective Brown. "C'mon, Abigail, you know I can't build a case on *maybe*. Do you have any physical evidence...like DNA?"

"Yeah, but it's inconclusive until we can get a sample from the suspect for comparison...he's not in any of our data banks. I recently caught sight of him and seized some of his personal property. It's being tested as we speak, but we've yet to find out where he's hanging his hat or if he will continue his killing streak."

Walker thought for a second. "Are there that many millionaires in this city? Would it be possible to conduct surveillance on those who might become his next victims?"

The lieutenant cut in. "There are way more than you'd think...and we're already stretched to our limit on manpower. Abigail and her crew are so close they can almost smell the perp's body odor. Give them another couple of days, and I think they'll serve up this guy as an appetizer for your promotion party."

"Let's not get ahead of ourselves, but keep me in the loop." Walker scoffed. "Promotion...I guess I'll have to learn how to be a politician after all...unless we botch this case. Then I'll find myself working in traffic court." He got up to leave. "Thanks, ladies, keep up the good work."

The ADA was no sooner out the door, when the Hun eyeballed Abigail. "He's a good egg...lets catch this bastard and get him promoted."

Abigail got up and headed for the door. "Aye-aye, skipper."

68
Itchy

I'm relaxing in a Lazy-boy recliner I scored from the neighborhood thrift store. It is one of three pieces of furniture in this abandoned building I call home. Besides the slightly used perfectly broken-in chair, there is an old two-drawer file cabinet that seconds as an end table. The third piece is a huge metal safe...must have been too big and heavy to move. A faded decal reads 'Bank of America' and is still visible on the door. Either a financial institution had occupied the space before the drug store, or the pharmacist purchased it second hand. It doesn't really matter.

What intrigues me is the false panel in the back of the safe, below the bottom shelf. Since the door doesn't close, let alone lock, the secret compartment is a perfect place to stash the rest of my cash and a few personal items I hold dear. I found the compartment by accident; I saw a mouse scratching at one corner and heard what sounded like a hollow space behind the metal.

Shifting in my seat, I move the crossword under the beam of natural light from the skylight above. The answers come too easy, but that's normal for most newspaper puzzles. Since the fall in newsprint popularity, I think editors simply pilfer and plagiarize material from other sources...just like fake news...the new norm.

4 down – rich. 16 across – entitled. 7 down – monetary. 18 across – arrogant. 12 down – powerful. The words echo in my head. There is a theme. Is it an omen? I get that hollow sensation in my stomach again...that itch I can't scratch. I haven't felt it in a while. The Jew jeweler appears in my mind. Clearly, there is a message in the answers to the puzzle. Neil Segal has to die.

The paper in my lap, I push the recliner all the way back and stare up at the dirty cumulous clouds drifting by the skylight. Some shapes bring back childhood memories...when life was much simpler. One resembling a man lying prone appears. Its movement gives him life. The cloud's deep hues resemble the colors of death...another omen.

It isn't just the thought of killing the jeweler. It's the pleading and tortured faces of my other victims that haunt me. I experienced plenty of my own suffering, but it's the misery I cause others that I can't shake. Is my guilty conscious winning the battle between revenge and redemption? Is it time to stop or is it time to kill again?

I thought about the police and the attractive bitch, Brown. Is she an avenger, sent to intercede on God's behalf and put an end to my killing spree? Is she a worthy opponent, whose mission is to challenge my murderous skills and level of determination? Someone to test my intelligence and resolve?

Contradicting thoughts block the images I thought I saw in the clouds. The sun wins over the sky, dispersing and drying up the ominous shapes and shadows. I stare into the blue, seeking guidance from a higher power, perhaps the source of my motivation, and what drives me. I search for a sign, something to point me in the right direction.

A high-altitude jet passes overhead. Just before it disappears from view, the sun's rays reflect into my eyes. Blinking to correct my vision, I focus on the empty sky once again. I feel the void within its vastness...an emptiness that burns and itches deep inside me...the itch to kill again.

69
Tags

Ackley Scott banged away on his keyboard, pulling up crime scene logs from every one of the millionaire murders. He skimmed the reports and used a notepad to list all the parked vehicles found in and around the area of the killings. There were several and it took him a few hours to go through all the paperwork.

Checking his list, the young detective decided to upload the information into Excel so he could use the software to cross-reference the data. While he was listing license plates recorded by police, he noticed an anomaly. Two different vehicles, at two separate crime scenes, donned the same tag. Further investigation revealed the duplicate plates didn't belong to either of the vehicles.

Normally, police would check the registration of a particular vehicle if it or its owner were under investigation. In this case, the cars were parked in the area of a crime scene. If the investigating detectives ran the tags, they would discover they weren't the correct plates and assume the vehicle was stolen...a measly misdemeanor offence of no consequence.

Scott felt a rush. Something he hadn't experienced since being restricted to a desk. He thought about coincidence...something his partner taught him not to believe in. His increased heart rate told him it was more than that. The odds were too great. What was the chance the same license plate would show up on different vehicles at two crime scenes in separate parts of the city?

70
Closing

Lynda Campbell and Karl Knudsen checked two post office locations to see if their key fit any of the boxes, but struck out at both. It was the third place, near the library in Mexican Town, where they found the winner. As luck would have it, the clerk on duty recognized the likeness of Elbert Fromm and confirmed he had a box there. She delivered the bad news. Fromm had been in earlier to empty the box and close his account. The clerk mentioned he didn't have his key and had to pay extra to have the box opened. Campbell asked how the fee was paid and the woman said he used cash—a new one-hundred-dollar bill.

The woman produced the paper note. The detective examined it closer and called Abigail Brown. "Abs, Lynn...we're at the post office in Mexi-town. Fromm closed out his box here and paid with a C note...serial number A944058. It's a new bill, does it line up with the others you seized?" She heard papers rustling on the other end of the line.

"Hang on...I have the list here somewhere...got it. A944...yup, it's the same series. You seized it?"

"Yes. And get this...the library he visited is only three blocks away. Looks like that geographic profile stuff really does work. We're heading over there next."

"Good work, Lynn. Let me know how you make out...gotta take another call." Abigail disconnected.

The B Team headed to the public library. Knudsen spotted the cute librarian from the front door and said he'd take the lead. He puffed his chest and proudly displayed his badge at the desk. The curly-haired brunette gazed over her reading glasses at his ID, and checked to see if his face matched the photograph. If she was impressed, he couldn't tell.

Signaling he was the man in charge, he asked the librarian if she could look at a photograph, and lightly elbowed his partner for her to produce it. The petite woman pushed her glasses up the bridge of her nose and examined the image.

"Yes, Detective, I recognize him. Can I ask why you are inquiring?"

Campbell started to reply but her partner cut her off. He leaned over the desk, and got close enough to count the woman's eyelashes. He was firm and direct. "This man's wanted for multiple murders, and we have information he used one of your computers to access the internet." The macho cop offered a wry smile. "We're concerned for your safety."

Knudsen's words landed hard and the bookworm straightened in her chair. "Oh my god, he looked so harmless. I did catch a peek at his search history...he likes to do puzzles on line. Seems quite good at it."

"You've spoken to him?"

"No, I have the ability to check on what library patrons are doing online...to make sure they're not watching or doing something improper or illegal. It was a site for complex puzzles and a chat room for gamers...that sort of thing."

Knudsen walked around to the side of the desk to check her out. She wore a dress. He did his best to imagine the parts that were covered. "Is there any way you can show us which sites he was on or bring up his search history?"

The librarian sensed her space being invaded, and rolled her chair further from the overbearing detective. She frowned. "I'm sorry. We clear the history and cookies every day to avoid viruses and possible hard drive corruption."

The male detective sensed he had entered her safe zone and took a step back. "Is there anything else you can tell us about the man?"

"Not really, I'm sorry. He never said much and seemed to come in at slow times, when no one else was around. Sometimes he stayed right until closing. If he didn't look so harmless, I might have worried about being alone in here with him. But now you've scared me...what should I do if he comes back in?"

He exchanged looks with his partner, and reached in his pocket and produced a business card. "My personal cell number is on here...call me anytime...whether he comes back, or not." Knudsen mustered the friendliest smile he could manage, to show his sincerity.

Campbell waited until they got back in the car. "Really, Karl? Were you trying to impress her or scare the crap out of her? Maybe you should have given her your home number too."

"C'mon, Lynda, you don't understand. It's a guy thing...you know...the sexy librarian?"

71
Geography

Abigail studied the map of Detroit and considered the geographic profile she put together. While in the military, working logistics in the desert could be difficult. Some cities remained stationary for centuries, but roads and sand dunes shifted daily with the wind. In an urban area like the Motor City, things were much easier. Detroit was laid out in a grid, and occurrences at particular addresses became raw data for a computer to ascertain specific crime patterns. Investigators could use that information to target or even predict criminal activity in selected neighborhoods.

During her stint with the FBI Behavioral Science Unit, Detective Brown also learned the art of criminal profiling. The methodology is about studying offender behavior and their crime patterns. It is a known fact many criminals tend to commit offences within the boundaries of their neighborhood. There are also disadvantages in using these techniques when trying to track someone like the millionaire murderer. Timing and crime scene behavior had to be taken into account. In this particular investigation, the suspect didn't seem to follow any schedule and used different modus operandi for each murder.

Abigail Brown felt confident their suspect, Elbert Fromm, was hunkered down somewhere in or around Mexican Town.

She narrowed the search to an area bordered by the Fisher Freeway, Livernois Avenue, and the railway tracks.

The lead detective spent most of the day scouring evidence reports from forensics and checking tips phoned in by concerned citizens. Aware of the manhunt, they hoped to cash in on the reward, offered by the governor himself. The allure of free cash always brought out the greediness in people, and it cost the department lots of man-hours answering the calls.

Abigail was tired of being an armchair quarterback. Keeping in mind the latest input from Ackley Scott about the license plate, and Lynda Campbell about the library, she grabbed a set of car keys and headed out. Like any other good cop, Brown knew that getting her hands dirty and working the street was one of the best ways to catch criminals in their own element. She needed to drive the grid and get a feel for the killer's nesting ground.

72
Determined

I consider myself a smart, but simple man. I never asked more from life, until life itself let me down. I was raised properly and did everything expected of me to earn my place in society. I've learned life is not always fair. Frankly put, I was dealt a shitty hand. Cards handed out by a wealthy and uncaring man, who sealed his own fate in his personal quest.

To me, a one-time budding pharmacist, Neil Segal is that type of man too. He uses and discards other people as if they are soiled toilet paper. Just how many jewelry stores does one person need? Is it not enough he drives a top-of-the-line Mercedes and lives in a huge mansion?

Coming from a modest upbringing, I have no idea what it's like to enjoy such luxuries. I was quite happy with the middle-class lifestyle of my parents, and expected my adult life would be lived in the same fashion. We were all content. It wasn't until our lives took a turn for the worse that I learned the importance of having money. Maybe it doesn't buy happiness, but it surely provides security.

After selecting a new set of wheels, I grab a license plate from the parking lot behind Xochimilco's Restaurant in Mexican Town. The Ontario tag is a no-brainer and is from the same make of minivan I'm driving. It isn't unusual to see Canadian plates in and around the Detroit area. There are plenty of them around the Mexican restaurants.

Leaving the familiarity of my newly adopted neighborhood, I drive east to Corktown, where Segal's newest Pristine Jewelers is located. I watch the man at his places of business now since the soup kitchen is off limits for me. After the demise of the old Tiger Stadium, the area is experiencing a resurgence of life, where young urban professionals move in to take advantage of low real estate costs, and new businesses plant roots to take their money.

I pull to the curb near the Starbucks. A patron leaves a parking spot vacant. The vantage point offers me a clear view of Segal's store, where the wealthy owner is working late. Counting all his money, no doubt. I'm not the sort of guy who normally pays for a fancy overpriced cup of mud, but I think the upscale coffee shop is the perfect place to break another C note...and I was curious to see what all the hubbub was about.

I sip a dark roast, keeping watch on the store across the street for any movement inside. I have never seen so many types and blends of coffee, and can't believe the ridiculous prices they charge for it. No wonder the young clerk never batted an eye when handed a hundred-dollar bill. The brew cost more than the shoes I wear, but it wasn't half-bad.

It isn't unusual for Segal to work late so I get comfortable and open one of my crossword books. Filled with quick and easy puzzles, I find it suits surveillance. I won't be too distracted. A cop cruiser double-parks out front of the Starbucks and a young oinker goes inside. They must have gotten a raise if they can afford the overpriced java.

My plan is to follow Segal home from work, where I can approach him in the garage and kill him. A few dry runs helped me work out the timing. After seeing the weasel drop off his wife at the airport yesterday, this is the perfect time to do the deed. The death I plan for him might be painless, but he will have plenty of time to suffer before he succumbs.

In keeping with my repertoire of cruel and varied methods of eradication, I choose carbon monoxide poisoning for Neil Segal. He will die in his own car, parked in his own garage, at his own house. Like all the others, the Jew will have a number...how ironic. Since the cops are getting closer, I'll make this one more difficult to find.

From everything I learn about Miss Brown, she is more than capable. I wonder if she has any of the numbers figured out yet. It really doesn't' matter. It obviously goes to motive, but they have to catch me for it to be of consequence. Another cop car stops in front of the Starbucks...an unmarked unit. The passenger exits to get a coffee. It's the female dick who was at the soup kitchen with Brown, the same bitch who questioned me before I vacated my home.

73
Retribution

Bruce Dunn wasn't enjoying his extended absence from police work. He talked his doctor into writing him a note for stress leave, an ailment hard to prove but easy to fake. No one from work dared to question him after nearly being shot to death. They respected the fact PTSD affected everyone differently. To him it was all about shitting the bed on the millionaire murder case.

The sidelined homicide detective had a plan. He could use the time off to conduct his own investigation into the high-profile case. Away from competition, and the detectives Dunn considered to be glory hounds. He could do things his own way. He lost an ally in the captain, but there were plenty of other important people who would be happy to see the serial killer brought to justice.

In reality, Dunn hoped to force the killer into a confrontation. He could take him out of the equation permanently and be a hero again. He snuck into the major crime's office at night, and kept up to date on the status of the investigation. Dunn learned Mike Connors was still in the wind. That was a mistake on his part, and it cost him his solid reputation.

That would all change now he knew everything his fellow detectives had learned about Elbert Fromm. He thought they should have caught the man by now. Obviously, he'd prove to them who was the better investigator. He always believed Abigail Brown's previous success was blind luck, but still bought into the methodology she used to profile the killer and his stomping ground.

Bruce Dunn had a few things going he thought would lead him to the killer first. He knew the streets well, having worked undercover in narcotics. He took a police radio so he could listen in on the investigations channel when his co-workers were out on the road. He even conducted his own surveillance on Detectives Brown, Campbell, and Knudsen. Knowing some of his co-workers' quirks and habits made it easy to predict their movements while they went about the business of conducting their investigation.

74
Hideout

Abigail Brown drove up and down the streets in Mexican Town, starting at the Fisher Freeway and working her way west. She checked the alleys, paying special attention to any abandoned buildings where Fromm might be hiding out. Cruising past the Mexican restaurants on Bagley, she wondered what the attraction was. To her, Mexican Village, on the other side of the freeway, had the best food.

There was nothing on 23rd, 24th, or 25th streets that caught her attention. There were abandoned and burnt-out crack houses, but the detective couldn't picture the millionaire murderer holed up in one of them. Was she overthinking it, and he was hiding somewhere in plain sight? He had access to stolen cash, and could certainly afford a hotel room. She thought not.

Brown stopped in front of a long-gone pharmacy on the corner of Bagley and West Grand Boulevard. The door and windows were boarded up, with evidence of a sign boasting the name of the business that once called the old building home. The letters were gone but a shadow remained; Boulevard Drugs.

Something clicked in Abigail's brain. She knew that pharmacy name. It was the place where Fromm and his father worked years earlier. It appeared the store had been abandoned for some time, but neglect and neighborhood vandals may have sped up the aging process. She thought of calling Ackley Scott to confirm the address but reversed, and drove down the alley instead.

The back door was recessed in an alcove, off the alley. It wasn't boarded over. Brown was about to drive on, but something felt odd, and she stopped. She got out of her car and checked the solid steel door. It was secure. Admiring the artistic graffiti, she noticed the clean area around the keyhole. There were scuffmarks in the dirt at her feet. Someone had used the door recently.

Abigail walked the perimeter of the building, looking for another way in. She couldn't find one. There was a fire escape on the back of the two-story building next-door. The detective climbed the stairs. From the top, she could see a skylight on the roof of the old drug store. The detective was able to use the landing on the fire escape to reach the adjacent roof. She stopped in front of the rooftop window.

Abigail felt something deep in her gut; her instincts. Her cop sense had kicked in. A few of the meshed panels were cracked but the glass was intact. Someone had gone to the trouble of cleaning the glass. She bent over and peered down into the abandoned building. Her heart fluttered. There was a recliner chair directly below the skylight. Taking a deep breath, she leaned in for a closer look. There were small stacks of newspapers near the chair.

Something she saw on the seat cushion caused every muscle in her body to go rigid. It was a book of crossword puzzles.

75
Found

Abigail's phone ringing startled her and she nearly lost her balance. She wondered if the old glass would have held her weight. She answered the call. Ackley said he had some good news but wasn't sure how it could bolster their case. Brown walked the perimeter of the roof to see if there was another way into the building. "What've you got, partner?"

"Smith and Jones found stolen jewelry from one of our victims at a pawn shop not too far from the soup kitchen where you saw Fromm."

"Don't tell me our mastermind sold it using his own name."

"No. It was a guy named Kenyatta Watts...has a lengthy record with us but no fixed address. The last time he was arrested, it was for outstanding warrants. Get this...he was picked up at the soup kitchen. Do you think Fromm has other street people selling stuff for him?"

"Who knows? Maybe he really is a Robin Hood. Anything else?"

"Maybe. I checked on the pawn shop...it's a chain owned by a numbered company...the same company that owns Pristine Jewelers...not that it means anything. You find anything out there?"

"Funny you should ask. You'll never guess where I'm at right now."

"How many guesses do I get?"

"None. I found Fromm's hideout. I'm standing on top of it right now."

"What does that mean...is he there?"

Abigail made her way down the fire escape next door. "I don't think so...I'm looking for a way to get into the building."

"You want me to send backup?"

Brown's phone signaled another call coming in. "I'll take care of it...another call's coming in. Catch you later." She recognized Lynda Campbell's number.

"Lynn, what's up?" She heard Campbell and Knudsen bickering in the car.

"I just grabbed a coffee at Starbuck's and..."

Abigail cut her off. "No, thanks, I'm in the middle of something else...I found the lion's den and I'm trying to..."

"Abs, it's not about coffee...I think I might have seen the lion." Knudsen still squawked loudly in the background.

"What...where? Shut your partner up and tell me what's going on." Abigail returned to her car in search of a tire iron.

"We've got a problem here. Karl says Bruce Dunn is tailing us and I thought I saw Fromm near the Starbucks. There's an Ontario tag on his van but I didn't catch the number. He was pretending to read a magazine while watching Pristine Jewelers, across the street."

76
Triathlon

Knudsen checked his rearview mirror as he drove around the block to get another look at the man Campbell believed to be Fromm. Brown was still on the phone, requesting her friend keep the line open. She asked for their location, told them to stay put, and said she was on the way. Lynda put her phone on speaker so Karl could listen in.

Abigail talked about Pristine Jewelers and how it was tied to a pawnshop where a victim's stolen property was recovered. She went on about the soup kitchen and Robin Hood. Her tone was frenzied. Campbell felt the rush too. She had a gut feeling the man in the minivan was indeed Elbert Fromm.

Knudsen entered the stretch of road where the jewelry store and coffee shop were located. His partner called out their progress to Brown while he swore under his breath about Dunn tailing them. Abigail asked why the off-duty detective was there but Lynda stopped her, saying they were about to pass by the suspect vehicle.

There are two things an experienced investigator should never do while conducting surveillance: drive by the target more than once, and make eye contact with the person you are watching. Detective's Campbell and Knudsen did both.

77
Escape

I am so tired of waiting for Segal to leave the store, I imagine him stepping out onto the street, where I can run him over, and be done with it. I finish my puzzle, turn the page, and change channels in my mind. I wonder about my current online game with the psycho, known as Jason.

I hear a car coming up behind me. I saw the same unmarked unit earlier at the coffee shop. Using the crossword book to shield my face, I peer over the top to check the occupants of the car. It's the same female detective. She turns her head just enough to let me know I've been recognized.

I let them pass and start the engine. They turn right at the end of the block. I pull from the curb. A blue Mustang blows by me and almost takes out my left front fender. I make a U-turn and head in the opposite direction, going west on Michigan Avenue.

I pick up speed to distance myself from the cops. When I cross Rosa Parks, another unmarked car flies by me, going east. Their detective cars all look the same. I'm sure they spotted me and called for backup. At Wabash, I see the first unmarked coming up fast behind me. Thinking I need to get off the main road, I hang a hard left on 14th Street.

Roosevelt Park is on the right. I shoot across the grass and drive south along the pathway in an attempt to lose them. The cops make the turn onto 14th so sharp the car is almost on two wheels. I chose the wrong vehicle to outrun five-O. I stomp on the minivan's gas pedal and start to lose control on the broken concrete. I leave the park and head south on 15th Street.

78
Undone

Conducting surveillance on his fellow detectives paid off for Bruce Dunn. He thought something was up when Campbell and Knudsen circled the block in Corktown. His suspicion was confirmed when Lynda radioed dispatch for backup, and called in a pursuit involving their homicide suspect.

He caught up to them on Michigan Avenue and hung back while he formulated a plan. As far as Dunn knew, the suspect hadn't seen him yet. He had to choose the opportune time to join in the chase. He knew his 5.0-liter Mustang could outrun almost any other car on the road, especially an old cop car with a million miles on it. When Campbell and Knudsen chased the minivan through Roosevelt Park, he simply kept his distance on a parallel street. Dunn had been in a few pursuits during his career, but never one where he could listen and watch from a distance, waiting for his chance to move in for the kill.

That would be the best outcome, he thought, to get into a shootout with the suspect and take him out. It would make him the hero once again. Dunn thought about the millionaire murders and wondered if the killer carried a gun or knife. He could plant his throwaway back up piece, if necessary, but it would look better if the man produced a weapon traceable back to him.

Abigail was so pumped; her ass barely touched the seat. And she wasn't even in the chase. She slowly gained on the action, pushing her old plain-clothes unit to the limit. Private donations and an increased city budget gave way to fancy new patrol cars but the investigations fleet was in a sad state of repair.

Brown monitored the police radio and her cellphone at the same time. Knudsen and Campbell were still squabbling, her calling out directions and him cursing Dunn. Abigail wondered what the off-duty cop was up to and why he was there. Had he been acting on his own the whole time, monitoring them and hoping to capture Fromm and claim the glory for himself? What an asshole.

Having access to the play-by-play action allowed her to take shortcuts, and catch up to the pursuit. Patrol cars were busy or a long way off so she wasn't sure how a takedown might unfold. If Knudsen and Campbell caught up to the speeding minivan, they would have difficulty stopping it without getting someone hurt. High-speed chases were outlawed for exactly that reason. They normally ended badly.

79
Crash

Bruce Dunn loved the sound of his roaring engine, and how the exhaust pipes cracked when he downshifted. It appeared that Knudsen and Campbell were gaining on Fromm but their piece of shit unmarked unit was gutless. Good thing they were only chasing a minivan. The Bulldog grew impatient lagging behind and anxiously awaited the chance to jump on the suspect's ass.

He almost caught up to his fellow detectives, but had to pass a car in front of him. The pursuit turned onto Bagley, and Dunn made his move. He gunned it and fishtailed around the slowpoke in front of him, quickly closing the gap on his co-workers. What happened next left him no time to react—he was moving too fast.

Lynda yelled, 'Look out!' but Karl had no time to take evasive action and avoid another car that cut them off. Their speed and the force of impact sent them careening into a row of parked cars. They sideswiped three of them before the resistance of metal on metal spun them around in the middle of the road. They ended up facing the opposite direction.

Campbell watched everything happen in slow motion. Just before their car came to a complete stop, she saw the front end of a blue mustang coming at them head on. Bruce Dunn was behind the wheel, wearing a wide-eyed 'oh shit' expression. Knudsen saw him to. He yelled, 'Mother Fucker!' a split second before the Bulldog's car plowed into them.

During the crash and resulting chaos, Campbell dropped the cell phone and portable radio. Stunned for a moment, she fumbled around between her feet and found the phone. Abigail was still on the other end of the line. She asked if they were okay.

Her partner had a gash on his forehead, was bleeding profusely, and appeared dazed. His condition didn't deter him. Knudsen almost ripped the driver's door off the hinges, forcing his way out of the car. He spewed profanity as he charged toward Dunn's car. Lynda told Abigail they lost the suspect, and she better hurry to their location before her partner kills the Bulldog.

80
Succeeding

Where did those fuckers go? The unmarked car was gaining on me but now it's gone. I circled the block and hid in a private driveway to see if the cops would drive by. They never did. I got out of the van and peeked over a hedge, checking down the road. I'm laughing inside. This is the most fun I'd had in years. I can see the cops are involved in a huge crash with other cars.

Who'd have thought the kid voted 'least likely to succeed' in high school would outwit the fuzz and become a famous serial killer? I've accomplished a lot since my father died. Maybe I should have told the old man I would avenge him someday.

The truth is none of this was planned. It seemed like a good idea at the time...an idea that blossomed into a full-time job. Too bad I don't get paid for it. Wait, that's not quite true, some of my victims have paid me to kill them. Ha-ha...that's funny. Who could imagine revenge could be this rewarding? Working on puzzles is fun, but this game is a blast.

I am sure the police will never catch me, but I must admit I worried for a minute...especially about that black female cop. Man, I'd like to get her naked and in handcuffs. Abigail Brown...I wonder if she'd go for a brainiac like me...under different circumstances. Such a waste...a hottie like her turning out to be the fuzz.

What a mess. Someone needs driving lessons. The blue mustang is involved in the crash too. He must be another cop...too funny...waste of a nice car.

I think it's time to dump this ride and get out of town. I need to get my stash first...for travelling money...Canada maybe. Thought I saw the top of the Ambassador Bridge earlier. Maybe I can grab a taxi and take it across the border. I doubt if they'll be looking for me over there...or would they? I can't afford to underestimate my favorite cop again. I wonder if she plays chess.

A plan is coming together. Stop at the hideout, get the cash, and ditch the van in one of the restaurant parking lots. I can grab a cab in front of one of the eateries.

Another peek down the road confirms the cops are tied up for a while. Even their sirens are absent. Are they that stupid, shouldn't they still be searching for me?

81
Choked

Having a front row seat and knowing what could happen, Abigail Brown was horrified watching the wild car chase from a distance. She played catch-up trying to keep Fromm in sight, but didn't engage in the daisy chain of cars chasing him. She hoped uniformed cars would eventually box the suspect in or cut him off. She heard sirens but they weren't close enough.

The seasoned detective wondered what his next move might be. Where is he going? Had he panicked, was he simply fleeing to avoid capture, or did he have a plan? Fromm was smarter than any serial killer she'd ever dealt with. Why was he so different?

So many more questions than answers...she'd have to catch him to find out. That's if another police officer didn't kill him first, or he did himself in. Brown hoped it wasn't going to be a suicide by cop. At that point, with the added tension of a high-speed pursuit, if he so much as reached for his cellphone, someone would likely take him out. It wouldn't be the first time.

When Abigail turned onto Bagley her muscles tensed, and her heart skipped a beat. A wave of emotions came over her...surprise, shock, sorrow, anguish. She'd seen too many bad collisions and human carnage. Brown expected the very worst when she saw what lay ahead. Suddenly Lynda's voice returned to the phone, and said they were okay.

Getting closer to the multi-vehicle pileup, Abigail noticed Dunn's Mustang. There were other wrecked cars on both sides of it. Campbell and Knudsen's unmarked unit was in front of Dunn's—they'd collided head on.

As she rolled up to the crash scene, Abigail saw Knudsen leaning into the Mustang, shouting at the driver. The Square Head had a grip on Bulldog's neck and it appeared as though he was trying to pull him out of his car through the open window. She'd seen an angry cop do it once before. They referred to it as being reborn, a delivery where it didn't end well for the driver. Abigail got out of her car and ran to Knudsen before he did something he'd regret.

Lynda arrived at her side and they tried to pull her partner off their fellow detective. She pleaded with Karl to let him go, while Abigail tried to free his grip from Dunn's neck. Maybe Knudsen noticed his coworker turning blue, or he realized he was strangling a fellow cop. He simply let go and stepped back.

Campbell pushed him further away, and turned to Abigail. "Go, Abs, he couldn't have gotten far...check with patrol, maybe they're on to him by now."

Abigail stood fast for a moment, her mind racing. She nodded and ran back to her car.

82
Noise

I'm adjusting my plan. I'll dump the van first and walk to my hideout. It will be easier to take cover on foot. I'm sure every cop in the city has a description of my vehicle by now. I'll try to stay off the street, use the alleys, and cut through back yards and vacant lots, to stay out of sight. I duck down in tall weeds surrounding an abandoned ball diamond. My heart is racing and I can feel the beads of sweat collecting on my forehead. A cruiser rolls by slowly, the heads of both cops on swivels. Dummies...maybe you should get your asses out of the car and look around.

Other than a stray cat chasing something through the grass, I didn't see another soul the rest of the way to my hideout. It's no surprise in that neighborhood, a victim of Detroit's mass exodus to parts unknown. If anyone still lived in the scattered homes, they were nowhere to be seen.

It's weird how the closer I get, the more anxious I become. It's completely different being the hunted, instead of the hunter. It's exciting but I'm uneasy not being in control. My fate is in the hands of the city's trigger-happy cops. They find it easier to gun someone down, rather than endure the inconvenience of appearing in court.

I'm in the alley near my hideout. I gawk up and down the street, making sure there are no cops steaking out the place. Nobody jumps out of the bushes to arrest me. I crouch behind an abandoned house across the way to take a closer look. All is quiet in the neighborhood.

I walk over to the old drug store, unlock the back door, and go inside. Something feels off, as if maybe someone has been in here, but everything is exactly how I left it. I'm sure because I'm anal that way. It drove my parents crazy. I sense movement above me, but it's only a pigeon pecking at bugs on the skylight.

Walking to the safe, I stop dead in my tracks. A noise outside catches my attention...the sound of tires rolling over crushed stone and broken glass in the alley. The noise stops. Did I leave that door unlocked? I had better check. Is that footsteps?

83
Surprise

Abigail broadcasted the suspect was still at large; last seen going west on Bagley in a grey minivan. Two different sector cars responded and said they were in the area. She laid out the perimeter where they should concentrate their search. Experience and a gut feeling told the seasoned detective the millionaire murderer was still in the area.

Hoping the patrol cars would do a street-by-street grid search; she decided to backtrack and check the places where Fromm had been seen. Brown drove through Mexican Town, checking parking lots and driveways for the suspect vehicle. She slowed to eyeball a few pedestrians, but none matched the killer's description. No doubt, he would be the person running in the opposite direction.

She'd already passed the abandoned drug store once, but went around the block to come up the alley. Another look at the back door and skylight surely couldn't hurt. The overgrown alley reminded Abigail of something in an apocalypse movie. Where the planet had been laid to waste, revealing only faint remnants of human civilization. Tall and unkempt weeds grew in ever-expanding cracks in the crumbling pavement. Block walls on decaying buildings were covered with tags and graffiti. The ground was littered with plastic bottles, broken glass, and other discarded artifacts from another era. Her car tires groaned and crunched debris. Abigail hoped she didn't get a flat tire. It wasn't the time or place. She looked at the back door of the old drug store. It appeared to be ajar.

The detective got out of her car for a closer look. Abigail sucked in air through parted lips and held her breath. She was right—the door was unlocked and partially open. Her years of military and police training kicked in. She had to call for backup; it was the smart thing to do. Fearing Fromm might be inside, and hear her at the door, Brown turned off her radio. She drew her weapon and thumbed her cell phone with the opposite hand. Abigail pressed her back against the wall, and whispered to the dispatcher. She explained the situation, and requested assistance.

Brown hung up the phone and tried to formulate a plan in her head. She'd done dynamic entries with both the army and police. The element of surprise worked best. The idea being it took time for anyone inside to react to the sudden intrusion. What if Fromm came through the door, while she was waiting for backup?

Not happy with her position on the hinge side of the door, Abigail made a move to cover the opening on the other side. She didn't make it. The door swung open, hit her gun, and knocked it from her hand. Fromm made his exit.

They stood face to face.

84
Shit!

The door is unlocked and ajar. I hear whispering outside. Is it the cops? Why haven't they barged in and arrested my ass. A million things are running through my mind—what about my money, should I shut the door or bust out of here and run like hell? I stand still and listen but don't hear anything. Is it just someone passing by?

I lean forward and peek through the opening but I see nothing but an empty alley. Curiosity gets the best of me. I push open the door to check. It slams into something. Shit! Abigail Brown is standing there, staring at me.

Frozen in time, our minds are connecting on a psychic level, each of us trying to read the other's next move.

Damn, she is one good-looking woman. Too bad she's a cop; one who is trying to decide which of us is going to have a shitty day. The fog of the moment lapses, and I notice her hands are empty. Her gun is on the pavement a few feet away.

Should I go for it, before she has the chance?

85
Scissors

Fuck! It's him.

Almost nose-to-nose, Fromm and Brown stared at each other, neither one daring to blink. Abigail knew the gun was somewhere behind her, but was afraid to look back, in case he saw and went for it. In her mind, she told him he was under arrest, but the words didn't come out. Neither spoke. It seemed like an eternity, and then everything happened very fast.

They moved on each other at the same time, Fromm trying to flee and Brown trying to affect an arrest. She attempted a tackle by hitting him hard and low but he turned sideways in an attempt to get by her. The momentum sent Abigail crashing into one side of the doorframe, and allowed him to almost get by.

She was now inside, and he was half-way out. Brown worried he saw the gun, and was going for it. She held on to his arm. Fromm wasn't a big man but he was wiry and almost slipped her grasp. Abigail folded his limb, trying to put him in an arm hold to gain control and handcuff him.

Fromm threw his other elbow back and struck Abigail on the bridge of her nose. The blow stunned her for a second and made her eyes water. As if he was drowning, the killer flapped his arms wildly, trying to fend off the persistent cop. She knew right then he wasn't a fighter but he was trying his best to escape. He dove for her gun.

Brown was on top of him before he hit the pavement. She saw to it that he hit hard, his face bounced off the broken cement. Follow-through sent her elbow smashing into the same hard surface. Favoring her side gave Fromm a chance to roll on top of her. Blood from a cut over his left eye leaked down his face.

The millionaire murderer wasn't trying to flee anymore. He put both hands around Abigail's neck and squeezed. Something was in her eye, blurring her vision...blood. It wasn't his—he must have broken her nose. She grabbed his arms but couldn't break his grasp on her neck. Abigail couldn't breathe, but she wasn't ready to call it quits. She never quit.

Brown swung her long legs up and over Fromm's head, locking him in a scissor hold. He loosened his grip for a second, and she sucked in some air. She squeezed her legs as hard as she could. It was a race to see who could choke out the other first. The determined detective didn't stop there.

She used her fists to hammer away at Fromm, landing blows on his arms, face, and head. Their eyes were locked in a death stare; a contest Brown had every intention of winning. Her opponent seemed to be weakening. She took the opportunity to wiggle her body closer to the gun. Her handcuffs were out of reach, behind her back.

Brown heard a siren in the distance, a welcome sound to every cop who's ever been in distress. Hopefully, they'd get there soon, in case Fromm got the best of her. His face changed from red to purple from lack of air. Unable to breathe, she figured hers was the same. Her gun was only inches away; it seemed like a mile.

Fromm heard the siren too and he twisted his head to locate the source. Abigail never let up. Building up her legs and stamina by running every day paid off. Ready to pass out, the killer released the grip on her neck, and pinched the inside of her thighs, trying to loosen her hold on him. It worked just enough he was able to break free.

While Fromm staggered to his feet, Abigail grabbed her gun. She was blind in one eye from her bloodied nose. His face was smeared with a mixture of blood and gravel. They locked stares again for a split second. The killer turned to run. A police car roared up the alley and blocked his path of escape. He turned back to Brown, who was on her feet with her gun pointed directly at him. The millionaire murderer had nowhere to go.

86
Mickey

Lynda Campbell rolled up as patrol officers took Fromm away. She'd hitched a ride to the scene, and climbed out of another marked unit.

Abigail was sitting in her car with the door open. Her feet were hanging out and she held a bloodied wad of gauze over her nose.

"You alright, Abs, did anyone call for paramedics?"

"No, I told them not to...it's only my nose...a patrolman gave me this from their first aid kit...the bleedings almost stopped."

"What the hell happened?"

"Fucker broke my nose."

"I can see that...I mean how exactly did that happen? You didn't wait for backup, did you?"

Abigail pulled the gauze from her nose and checked for fresh blood. "Didn't gimme a chance to...crashed the door into me when I tried to cover the exit...knocked my gun out of my hand and the fight was on." She tilted her head toward the building. "We got down and dirty and tried to choke each other out. Patrol showed up and game over. Fudd was fucked."

"He went for your weapon?"

"Not at first...looked like he was trying to bolt past me. He's not much of a fighter, but wiry and gave me a good go."

Lynda shook her head and put a hand on her friend's shoulder. "Not a fighter, just a killer. But you got him, Abs. Way to go, girl!"

She nodded in acknowledgment. "Where are your partner and that dickhead, Dunn?"

Campbell scoffed. "Karl's okay...nice gash on his forehead...small in comparison to the size of his noggin. Dunn's screwed for sure. Patrol Sergeant started in on him, and the LT showed up and tore him a new one. Speaking of the Hun, here she comes now."

Their boss pried herself out of an unmarked unit and waddled over to the female detectives. "You okay, Crunch? Heard you nabbed our killer...I knew you could do it. Captain was on the phone to the mayor before Fromm even made it to holding." She leaned in for a closer look at Brown's nose. "That nose looks nasty...you aught a see a doctor. Soup can finish up here. Anything else you need?"

Abigail motioned to the building. "I haven't been in there yet...that's his hideout. We should get a search warrant."

"I can take care of that and call the ADA. Patrol can stay here to secure the scene. Soup and Square Head can do the search...he should be here soon. Like you, he refused medical attention. Seems I've got a squad full of tough guys and heroes. Well, except for one dumbass who won't be with us much longer. What the hell was he thinking?"

Abigail checked the gauze again, and tossed it to the ground with the other litter. "If it's all the same to you, LT, I'd like to stick around and see this thing through. Just keep Fromm on ice, and I'll interview him later. Maybe we'll find something to hold over his head...would be nice to bolster the case with new evidence."

The Hun puffed out her lower lip and exaggerated a nod. "Whatever you need, Detective. In case nobody else says it, "Great job today."

Campbell made her friend describe the arrest again, play by play, while they waited for the warrant. After the adrenaline stopped pumping through Abigail's veins, she felt a sense of calm, and satisfaction. After all, she just captured a serial killer; one that would no doubt, make a good case study at Quantico.

The women were discussing the images Simon described to Brown, when Knudsen pulled up. He wore a big bandage on the left side of his forehead, and carried a piece of paper in his hand; a search warrant. He eyed Abigail. "Way to go you wily wabbit, you captured Elmer Fudd. Looks like you should've ducked quicker."

Campbell punched her partner on the upper arm. "Look in the mirror, Karl, your booboo's bigger than hers?"

He rubbed his bandage. "I could have a concussion."

Abigail piped up. "On top of the brain damage you already have?"

Knudsen was about to respond but his partner cut in. "C'mon you two, lets search this place and see what Fromm has been keeping from us."

It didn't take long to search the building since there was nothing in it except for a couple pieces of furniture and an old safe. Abigail sat in the recliner and leafed through Fromm's papers and puzzles. She glanced up at the skylight, reliving the fight in her head. Knudsen kicked at the side of the safe, miffed since there was nothing in it.

Campbell shrieked and jumped back. "There's a dead rat in there."

The Square Head crouched down for a closer look at the rodent. "It's only a mouse...and lots of mouse shit...looks like he's been living in there."

Abigail walked over to see what had Lynda so excited. She looked over Knudsen's shoulder. "What's that little hole in the bottom corner...is that the mouse's house?"

Karl used his knuckles to knock on the metal. "Sounds hollow." He banged the panel with his fist and it popped open. "Well, lookie here..."

All three of them had their faces in the safe. The Square Head reached in and pulled out a nest made of shredded and chewed up one-hundred-dollar bills. He turned to the women. "Mickey Mouse was rich...do you think Elmer Fudd killed him?"

Later

Captain Zawadski took credit for closing the millionaire murders investigation. The mayor was ecstatic his supporters were safe again, and would happily contribute to his re-election campaign. Once the dust settled the chief of police transferred Zawadski to the traffic enforcement branch. When he made the move, he couldn't find his 18-year-old bottle of single malt scotch.

Harry Cummings took one day at a time, drying out and recovering from his injury. After collecting his pension, he took up an offer in Florida where he became the head of security at a marina near Palm Springs.

Bruce Dunn was never called a hero again. The DA declined to charge him for his involvement in the high-speed chase and resulting collision. The department however suspended and demoted him for numerous rules and regulations he blatantly ignored. He was transferred to the traffic branch where he worked for Captain Zawadski.

Karl Knudsen photoshopped an image of Abigail Brown and Elbert Fromm duking it out. The caption read, "I fought the law and the law won." He made several copies and posted them all over the police station. Because of his place on the promotion list, he was elevated to the rank of sergeant.

Lynda Campbell visited Simon again but she couldn't convince Abigail Brown to go with her. After Knudsen's promotion, she was left without a partner and the Hun decided to team her up with her best friend. She and Abigail became Detroit's first pair of female homicide detectives.

Jamila Harris celebrated Fromm's capture by having a three-course meal catered in for her crime unit. She passed around shots of single malt scotch and made a toast to Abigail Brown. The Hun took on the acting rank of captain to fill Zawadski's position. Harris continued with Weight Watchers but never seemed to lose any weight.

Ackley Scott finally asked Martha Wells out. She accepted. Given her poor choices in the past, she chose brain over brawn. Scott remained a deskbound ranger, and was disappointed by the partnering of Brown and Campbell, but he thought the women made a good team. His little brother, Justin, became the undisputed champion in the online game room.

Elbert Fromm refused to confess and asked for a lawyer. He was represented by the best legal aid lawyer a lack of money could buy. The high-priced lawyers that normally jumped on such cases steered clear for fear of losing any of their rich clients. The Millionaire Murderer was sentenced to ten consecutive life sentences with no chance of parole.

Abigail Brown was invited back to Quantico to present the Fromm case, and share his unique criminal profile. She passed up the opportunity to write the sergeants exam, once again. Her and Lynda continued their celebration after the Hun's victory meal. They got drunk in Greektown and Abigail texted Norm Strom.

About the Author

Edmond Gagnon grew up in Windsor, Ontario, Canada. He joined the Windsor Police Department in 1977, a month before his nineteenth birthday. After almost two years as a police cadet, Ed was promoted to Constable and walked a beat in downtown Windsor. He spent the next thirteen years in uniform, working the street.

From there, he transferred to plain clothes where he worked in narcotics, vice, property crimes, fraud, and arson. He was promoted to Sergeant, then Detective. During that time, Ed investigated everything from theft and burglary to arson and murder. He retired with a total of thirty-one years and four months of service.

Within weeks of retirement, Ed took to travelling the world, visiting countries in Southeast Asia and South America as well as riding his motorcycle all over Canada and the United States. He kept in touch with family and friends through email, sending them snippets and stories of his adventures.

The recipients of his musings suggested he write a book about his travels and Ed put together a collection of short stories in his first book, *A Casual Traveler*. Bitten by the writing bug, Ed decided to share some of his police stories.

He created the Norm Strom Crime Series, inspired by events and people he encountered during his years in law enforcement. In that series, Ed wrote and self-published *Rat, Bloody Friday, Torch, Finding Hope, Border City Chronicles,* and *Trafficking Chen*. He also started the Abigail Brown Crime Series with, *Moon Mask*.

Edmond Gagnon continues to write, adding *The Millionaire Murders* to his Abigail Brown Crime Series. *Border City Chronicles – West Side Stories* is already in the works. He also wrote a science fiction thriller called, *Four*. Ed still travels frequently and resides in Windsor, with his wife, Cathryn.

You can see all of Edmond Gagnon's books and more at:
www.edmondgagnon.com

Other Books by Edmond Gagnon

Norm Strom Crime Series
Rat
Bloody Friday
Torch
Finding Hope
Border City Chronicles
Trafficking Chen

Abigail Brown Crime Series
The Moon Mask
The Millionaire Murders

Others
Four – A Paranormal Thriller
A Casual Traveler
(A Collection of Short Travel Stories)

Website: www.edmondgagnon.com

CPSIA information can be obtained
at www.ICGtesting.com
Printed in the USA
BVHW051921230922
647846BV00001B/17